NASH

The $ecret Billionaire $ociety

BOOK 2

NANCY PENNICK

The Secret Billionaire Society series is dedicated to my family who have loved, helped and supported me through this process.

The $ecret Billionaire $ociety
(Contemporary Romantic Suspense)

Chase (Book 1)

Nash (Book 2)

Finn (Book 3)

Beau (Book 4)

Gabe (Book 5)

Kade (Book 6)

The Elusive Mr. Smith (Book 7)

Smith's Revenge (Book 8)

BEFORE YOU GO

THANK YOU FOR READING

Did you enjoy this book?
I invite you to leave a review at your favorite book site, such as
Goodreads, BookBub and Amazon.

DID YOU KNOW THAT LEAVING A REVIEW…

Helps other readers find books they may enjoy.
Gives you a chance to let your voice be heard.
Gives authors recognition for their hard work.
Doesn't have to be long. A sentence or two about why you liked the book will do.

OTHER BOOKS BY NANCY PENNICK

Waiting for Dusk Series (Young Adult)

Waiting for Dusk (Book 1)

Call of The Canyon (Book 2)

Stealing Time (Book 3)

Taking Chances (Short Story)

Broken Dreams (Prequel)

Twenty Nine Series (Young Adult)

29

29 Squared

29 Degrees

29 Forever

The Clan MacLaren Series (Historical Romance)

My Highlander Husband (Book 1)

Donnach's Daughter (Book 2)

The Heart of the Emerald (Book 3)

Now and Forever (Book 4)

MacLaren Strong (Book 5)

Homecoming (Book 6)

ABOUT THE AUTHOR

Nancy Pennick, author of young adult and romance books, has been writing nonstop since retiring from teaching. Starting off as a young adult author, she has enjoyed diving into other genres. In other words, she likes to write whatever comes to mind! Born and raised in Northeast Ohio, she resides in Mentor, OH. Nancy is married and has one son.

PROLOGUE

"Mr. Nash Gill?" the voice said over the speakers.

"Present and accounted for Mr. Smith!" I raised my hand like I remembered Chase had when he was given the first assignment. He was the leader of our group, although he hated to admit it, and I followed his lead. "Yes, sir. I'm ready for duty. Cue the music."

I expected the *Mission Impossible* theme song to start up but only heard the breathing of my buddies around me.

"Be serious, Nash," Chase's voice came from behind me.

I could be serious as the next guy, but what was life without a little fun? My motto had been live fast and furious until I met these five guys in college. I passed up a football scholarship to attend Harvard and thank goodness I did. Not every guy made it to the NFL, and I'd been smart enough to realize it. My dream had always been the same since middle school, own a gym. Back then, I oddly thought I'd work out for free and hang with the customers. The older I got, I realized I needed business skills, networking and marketing experience. Where else better to learn the ropes than Harvard?

My roommate was a great guy from the New York City area, Beau Miller, and we'd quickly made friends with Chase Young and Finn Larsson who lived down the hall. Finn was from California, a rich guy's son, who wanted out from under his daddy's shadow, and Chase was driven to become something even back then. We added Gabe and Kade to the group sophomore year, and we'd been tight ever since.

Chase had been the first to see my potential, encouraging me to follow my dream of opening a fitness center in Miami. I owned a chain of them now, Gill's Gym, in Florida and one in Charlotte, North Carolina, Chase's hometown.

In fact, I was in Charlotte now. I sat in the bunker, as we called it, a place Chase had built on his property in North Carolina. Actually, it was a glorified man cave, the outer room filled with manly toys and the inner sanctum, where only the six were allowed, looked like an interrogation room with a one-way mirror and two rows of seats. We'd entered the room as a unit when Mr. Smith came to call.

Who in the hell was Mr. Smith? We had no idea. I thought back to our thirtieth birthday bash, all celebrated on the same day, an annual tradition since we graduated from college and went our separate ways. We'd come from all parts of the country to attend Harvard and on our birthday, no one could keep us apart. Thirty was big, or as I'd heard it called, Dirty Thirty. Had no idea why, but I liked it. Turning the big three-o got us thinking. What had we done with our lives?

We'd formed the Secret Billionaire Society as a joke during our junior year at Harvard, swearing we'd all be one by the time we reached thirty. To our surprise, it happened sooner rather than later, thanks to Chase's investment skills and Finn's ties to people with money and connections. The three of us were the first to agree to the made-up club. I dragged Beau into the society kicking and screaming. He insisted he'd reach the big time without us. But once he heard the pledge, we'd help each other no matter the circumstances, he was in.

Kade and Gabe were the creative types and didn't care about money in college. Then, they came to their senses. To follow their dreams, they needed cash or investors and jumped in feet first. Or headfirst? Whatever.

I learned to slow down but never gave up having a good time. I also despised being looked at as a jock because I worked out and liked it. Two lines of Chinese script tattoos ran down the inside of one bicep which made some think I was vain, all about the body and the look. Maybe a day's worth of stubble didn't help either. I shrugged it off long ago. No one, except these guys and my ex-girlfriend, knew I was a big softie inside.

On the fateful thirtieth birthday night, we drank, sang and reminisced until one in the morning. All went well until someone had gotten melancholy and asked if this was all there was to life—partying, drinking and making money. I stood, beer in hand, and gave quite the speech about the qualities of those three exact things. Someone threw wads of alcohol-soaked napkins in my direction as I broke into song. After the fight had calmed, we stared at each other for the longest time. It became the lightbulb moment. Beau did some research and Mr. Smith was born. The man behind the mirror. We'd never met him. We didn't know what he looked like. Yet, we'd agreed to put our lives in his hands and trust him.

We only knew his name—Mr. Smith. He was now in charge of us. He'd receive all we owned if we did not follow through with the assignments. That became our motivation, get our money back from him. If one failed, we all did. We thought Smith had selfless goals when we hired him early the next morning, spouting how much he liked our talk of doing something for the greater good. He promised to fit the assignments into our lives. Maybe he didn't have selfless goals after demanding our assets go into a trust. He might end up with all our money, but the Society agreed we wouldn't quit the project. We'd succeed no matter what.

During the birthday night, I found the *Mission Impossible* theme song and kept playing it during key moments. I thought it added suspense, but someone, no make that two guys, had to wrestle my cell away and threw it into another room. Couldn't a guy have a little fun? Sure, this was serious, we might have to start over again financially if we didn't complete our missions. Yet at five in the morning, no one seemed to care about the money. For a birthday bash, we'd gotten way too serious on how to save the world or let us get real … one person. Money be damned. I had liked the partying mood we'd established earlier in the night and wished to get back to it.

Before ending the call with Mr. Smith, the six of us had been instructed to put together dossiers. A special courier would retrieve the drives on a set day and deliver them to Smith. Once he had the memory stick in hand, he'd know everything about us. The only thing we asked was to give each of us a separate assignment. He'd set the parameters, make the rules.

After Smith received and read our bios, another courier would deliver the next set of instructions. Mr. Smith took no chances and didn't want us to use our cell phones, email, texts, or any technical means of communication to contact him. The first message we received had been to construct a soundproof room where we could meet, and the bunker was born.

Once built, we'd get our assignment and instructions in the room plus a burner phone, like

Chase had, whenever we needed to speak to the man. Smith had already tweaked the rules for my mission after speaking with Chase. The rest of us could keep our real phones, besides the burner, a lesson learned from the first assignment.

"Mr. Gill?" The voice called to me again.

CHAPTER ONE

Vanessa Alverez always came to work early when Nash was out of town. "Good morning, my little Pepita!" She walked to her lovebird's cage kept in the corner of her office. "Rise and shine."

A recognition chirp came from the little green bird with an orange head as it scrambled around the outer rim of the cage to get to the corner. Vanessa met the bird, giving it a treat. "Nash says I spoil you, but he's not the boss of me." She laughed.

Vanessa let out a breath. "I swore I wouldn't talk or think of him in that way again … like a boyfriend. Hard to do since his face is plastered all over the gym." She rolled her chair back and sat.

The last time they'd spoken, Nash had been in the Miami airport. He'd called one more time to ask her to reconsider their breakup. "We tried twice, Nash. Isn't that enough?" she had told him. "We have different goals in life. You already have yours and I plan to follow mine."

Nash had turned thirty, and Vanessa was close behind. Her dream of opening her own gym or running one of Nash's was slowly fading. Every time he'd plan a new franchise, she dropped hints she'd be the perfect candidate. She'd saved her money and had enough for the down payment, but it fell on deaf ears.

The newest Gill's Gym would open in Charlotte, North Carolina soon, home to one of his best friends, Chase Young. Vanessa never thought Nash would go outside of Florida but saw it as her opportunity. Sure, they'd be a few states apart, but Nash came to Charlotte so often, it was his second home. He even had a suite at Chase's home in the suburbs.

This time, instead of dropping hints, Vanessa asked outright for the job. Nash looked at her with his beautiful, honey brown eyes and said, "I've already got three perfect candidates, Van. You know me, I want to help guys out."

Guys was the key word. When it came to awarding franchises, women never made it to the final rounds. Nash had a big heart and tried to help those who couldn't achieve their dreams. She loved that about him. This time, his three candidates included a war vet, a high school teacher and a well-known boxing trainer who escaped from Cuba.

"Ugh!" Vanessa ran her hands through her dark hair, pulled it into a high ponytail and wrapped a band around it. "Pepita, am I invisible?" A chirp confirmed otherwise, making her laugh. "Maybe he won't admit it, but Nash wants me to work with him forever." She made a noise in her throat and folded her arms. "Men! I've wasted enough time thinking about him. Time to work out before we open."

Vanessa liked to get her workouts in when she had the place to herself. She needed to beat the five-thirty a.m. opening and tried to head down by five. Sometimes, Nash joined her, but even he knew she preferred silence. No televisions or music blaring, no ear buds or headphones, just quiet. A time to think and reflect.

Twenty minutes in, she heard the door unlock. Staring straight ahead, Vanessa refused to look Nash's way. She knew it was him by the grumbling noises he made as he tried to remove the keys from the door.

"I keep telling you to get a new lock or maybe a new door," Vanessa called. Determined to finish her treadmill run she kept a steady pace and eye on the wall.

A gym bag dropped in front of the treadmill and Nash leaned on the front of the equipment. "New outfit?"

"I always wear this on Monday." Vanessa wore a black halter trimmed in purple piping. The tight capris had two purple racing strips down the sides. Purple Nikes finished the look.

"Well, it looks new."

"Maybe you never noticed before."

"Are you almost done? We need to talk."

Vanessa slowed the machine. "Personal or business?" *Don't look him in the eye!* Her heart flipped when she did. The rugged man standing before her had the ability to melt her into a puddle of pliable goo and she wasn't going to let it happen.

"Business. Come to my office after your shower." Nash leaned forward and sniffed. "You could use it."

Vanessa grabbed a towel off the bar and swung it his way before wrapping it around her neck. "Ass."

"Are you going to use the peach perfume I like?" Nash wiggled his brows.

"I keep telling you it's not perfume, big guy. I don't buy the stuff. It's Peaches and Cream body wash and lotion. That's all."

"Right. Peaches and cream." Nash pointed at her. "A heavenly smell."

Vanessa closed one eye. "You're sure this is about business because I have a lot to do today."

"Trust me, it is."

Vanessa hadn't notice at first, but Nash looked like he was carrying a heavy burden as he ran a hand through his wavy brown hair. "You okay?"

"Yeah, like always. I'll open the doors for the early gym rats then head up to my office. Anyone else check in yet?"

"Nathan's in the back, Missy's in the office ready to check people in and Juan is opening the juice bar. They're all I've seen, but I'm sure the rest are here somewhere."

"You get in the zone when you work out, don't you, Peaches? Better be careful. Someone might sneak up on you."

Nash reached out to caress her cheek as she stepped from the treadmill. Vanessa swatted his hand away. "Don't."

"What?" Nash turned his hands over, palms up. "We can still be friends, joke around?"

"No!" Vanessa let out a breath. "Yes, we can. I'm tired of trying to make you see me as more than a girlfriend or a woman who works here. You went to Harvard, Nash. Women were in high positions at the college and the women students had goals. Goals beyond being someone's girlfriend. I have a business degree from Florida State. I'm just as good."

"Hey, give me a break! I'm not like that. You're putting words in my mouth. I never said you're not good enough because you didn't go to Harvard. You're second-in-command here. The assistant CEO."

"Right." Vanessa mumbled. *Hopeless as always. Useless conversation.*

Nash took her by her forearms, brought her to him and kissed her forehead. "I'm sorry you feel that way. When I look at you, all I see is my girl, the one I love and want to protect with my life."

"There's nothing wrong with that," Vanessa answered. "I love you feel that way. It's …" She pushed him away. "Never mind. I'm done explaining. Would you please move? I want to shower before it gets busy in here."

"Hey, we're not done," Nash called after her as Vanessa walked away. "See you in my office for round two."

In her office Vanessa had her own private bath and shower. She slammed her door closed and went into the well-appointed room. Flashbacks of Nash humming to her in the shower then playfully sniffing her afterwards to check if she was clean. "Stop it, Vanessa," she scolded herself, reaching for her body wash. She turned on the shower and stepped inside. "He's a child inside a man's body. When he decides to get serious, I'll be gone."

The day before, Vanessa had received a call from her mom, Renata. She'd invited Vanessa and her sister Rosa's family to come for a visit and stay at the gorgeous Chase Young compound. They'd be flown in tomorrow in his private jet and land at his C.Y. airlines facilities. Her mom was his house manager, having left Miami five years ago to work for him and rarely left the place. "You stole her away from us, Chase Young."

Vanessa turned and let the water beat on her back to get out the frustration she felt. She knew she shouldn't be angry with her mom or Chase. She loved them to pieces. When things went wrong with Nash, nothing seemed right in the world. "But I'd never tell him." She turned around, pushing her dark locks from her face.

Her hand hovered over the handle then she grasped it, turning the knob to cold for an icy blast and shut it off. She toweled off and dried her hair, letting it hang free, then remembered she had voicemails to answer.

"Business first, Nash," she said as she pulled the light gray polo embroidered with Gill's Gym in bright orange over her head. She slipped on gray gym shorts with orange strips and orange Nikes.

Vanessa had helped Nash choose the colors for Gill's, having been part of the business before they broke ground. She suggested pale gray walls with one side painted bright orange to make the rooms pop. The hardwood floors with orange tones fashioned winding paths through the gym. The design team had covered the workout areas in a dark gray industrial carpet made for heavy traffic. Large windows let in natural light and the customers had a landscaped view of palm trees and tropical flowers to enjoy as they worked out. The curved walkways through the gym broke up the rectangle-shaped rooms. The boxing ring in the smaller back room even had orange ropes. All her doing. Her ideas.

Hired as Marketing Director, Vanessa had always worked closely with Nash's best friend from college, Beau Miller. He was the go-to guy, the techie, the one who designed the gym logo. She never understood the little pyramid instead of a dot over the "i" in Gill's but had to admit it looked cool.

Beau's message had come in on her machine last night. She strolled to her desk and made a few clicking sounds at Pepita before sitting down. The little bird perked up at the noise and followed Vanessa's every move.

"You be quiet while I talk to Beau, Pita. No screaming." She heard his phone ring and he picked up on the third one. "Beau, what's up?"

"Hey, Vanessa."

She heard him breathing, but Beau said nothing else. "Beau?"

"Yeah, I'm here."

"You left the message, so here I am, returning the call."

"I saw Nash this weekend at Chase's. He said you two broke up. I wanted to see if you're all right."

"That's sweet, Beau, but I'm tough."

"From the way you sound, you didn't want to break up."

"He gave the franchise to the army vet, Beau! He doesn't see me as someone who's capable of running one of his businesses. I'm his little side piece."

"Whoa! Hang on there. I never heard him call you that."

"We've had this conversation before. You understand what I mean."

"I've tried to talk to him, Van. It's like he doesn't hear me."

"When it comes to me, he never does. It's always the same. I love her. I need to protect her. She can't go anywhere without me by her side or she'll fall down and hurt herself."

"Again, you're making that up. I never heard him say the last part." Beau chuckled. "I have an idea. Why don't I come for a visit? I'll tell Nash we need a face-to-face for business reasons, and I'll see what the big guy is thinking."

"Would you? I haven't seen you since we were at Chase's in May."

"Your mama was happy you're coming for a visit. When do you leave?"

"You talked with her?"

"Truthfully? Yeah, I was there this weekend with the guys. That's when Nash told me you broke things off."

"Oh, you guys can't seem to go longer than a month without seeing each other."

"It just happens, I guess. We don't keep track of the days. But, back to you. I'm sure a private jet is being sent down to Miami."

"Yes, we leave tomorrow, but I plan to come back Thursday. Rosie can stay as long as she wants with her family. I have things to do."

"Then I'll try to come to Miami on Friday. I could use some R and R."

"How long will you stay?"

"It might be a day trip. I'm not sure yet."

"Okay. Keep in touch. I've got a business meeting with Nash and need to tell him I'm leaving for a few days. He'll have to take care of Pepita while I'm gone."

Beau gave a hearty laugh. "He'll love hearing that. I'll text, Van. If I can't make it Saturday, it will definitely be next week."

Her spirits lifted after talking with Beau. She'd known him for six years now, being twenty-four when she started work at the gym. Vanessa sighed, remembering how impressed she'd been that twenty-five-year-old guys had such ambition. Each had made the top one hundred U.S. billionaires' list over the last three years. Beau had even reached his dream of being one of the top ten black billionaires in the United States.

Over the years, she'd learned Chase was the catalyst, the leader of the band of friends. At times, they were secretive, and she felt somewhat left out. But, when they were together as a group, everyone was friendly and they always had a good time, be it Miami, New York or Charlotte.

"It's about time you showed up," Nash growled when Vanessa appeared in his doorway. "Sit."

Vanessa sank into the chair across from him. "Can I …?"

"No," Nash grumbled. "Let me have my say first."

"Okay."

"Terrell Fisher deserved the franchise in Charlotte. He's a decorated army vet, served time in Southeast Asia and had to overcome PTSD. Terrell wanted a fresh start. Those are some of the reasons he got the job, Van. He's also got great business sense and agreed to oversee the project from the ground up without me holding his hand. It's his baby now."

"Nash, I'm aware you want to help out vets and minorities. That's well and good. I'm proud of you." *I fit in one of those categories! See me! Help me!*

"Thanks, but I'm giving the best man the job I believe." Nash leaned back in his gray leather high-back office chair and rocked. "Do you remember the other candidates?"

"Yes, Victor Dorado and Derreck Mills."

"I'm going to help them out, too."

"They're getting franchises?" Vanessa almost jumped out of her seat, longing to wring Nash's neck.

"Calm down." Nash held up a hand. "I said I wanted to help them, not give them franchises. We never got to discuss their resumes. You were too busy breaking up with me."

"Fine." Vanessa exhaled. "Tell me about them."

"Let's start with Victor. The plan is to hire him here, have him work in the boxing room. In Cuba, he was a highly regarded trainer. Now, after escaping, he lives with a brother here in Miami. I knew he'd never move. That's why I didn't give him the Charlotte franchise. Victor wants to get his wife and son out of Cuba, and it's best done from here."

"If I remember correctly, his son is a famous boxer there?"

"Yes, and Victor was his trainer. He ran a popular boxing camp in a rundown building for years, fixing it up as he made money and offered jobs to those in need. He made one mistake. Victor's too good at what he does. A criminal element moved in on him and his business."

"To escape, he had to do it alone. Undercover." Vanessa shook her head. "They'll never let his son and wife leave."

"You're right," Nash answered. "I plan to help him become what he was in Cuba, a well-known trainer. I'll find an up-and-coming boxer in his son's weight division and hopefully set up a fight here in Miami soon."

"Good luck! It's so far-fetched, I can almost see you pulling it off."

"Money talks, Van."

Her heart did a flip. Nash would put his money on the line for someone he recently met, making her love him all the more. "I want in, Nash, and don't try to stop me."

CHAPTER TWO

Nash cringed. He half expected Vanessa to say she'd help. *Why did I give her so much information?* "I won't try to stop you, but this may take time." *Two weeks is all I have.*

"I know who is ready for a fight, and he's not happy with his present trainer," Vanessa said, her eyes lit with excitement. "It has to be someone with credibility and worthy of an opponent, right? This guy is perfect … if they're in the same weight class."

"The purse tied to the event is a biggie, too. How much do you think I should throw in?" Nash chuckled as he watched her sit back to think.

The wheels spinning in Vanessa's mind had always been a turn on. She'd wake him in the middle of the night and deliver a new idea as clear as day. Afterward, they'd make love. He wanted those days back, but she seemed determined to stop every advance he made.

"Millions, but you'll make it back." Vanessa winked. "You always do. You didn't answer me. What's the son's weight class?"

"Lightweight."

"This was meant to be, Nash. I'll make some calls and get C.J. here. He's about one-hundred forty and fits what you need. I won't be here to get things started, but you'll be fine."

"Wait! You're leaving?"

"For a few days. Mama misses her girls. Chase is flying us up to Charlotte for a few days. I'll be back Thursday."

"That's what you wanted to tell me?" Nash lifted his brow in thought, recalling a conversation Chase had with Renata regarding a phone call she'd gotten from Miami. It was about him and Vanessa, he was sure.

Renata wouldn't come to Vanessa, so her daughters went there. He rubbed his face before he dropped his news. "I won't be here, either."

"What? Why?"

Darn Smith! I can see why Chase seemed aggravated all the time. He messes with your head and your life. "I need to go to Pennsylvania."

"Did I hear you right? *Pennsylvania.*" Vanessa folded her arms over her chest. "Why would you go there?"

"Derreck Mills."

"The other guy who didn't get the job? What's going on, Nash?"

"I told you there was something about these three guys. They need my help."

"What part of P.A.?"

"Pittsburgh."

"Does Pittsburgh get a Gill's gym?"

If Vanessa kept peppering him with questions, he was afraid he might tell her everything, yet Nash didn't want her to leave his office. He needed to leave soon and had no idea when he'd get back. Vanessa flipped her head and dark hair spilled over her shoulder down to one breast. Nash loved the silky feel of her hair and skin. *Not the best time to tell her.*

"Nash? Does Pittsburgh get a gym?"

"Um, no. I'm not sure yet."

Derreck's mission was the easier of the two. Nash had made his plan on the flight home. Fly to Pittsburgh, meet up with the coach and go to the high school where he worked. Nash wanted to see if there was land close by for the new gym. Kids could walk there after school. He'd have his crew on it in a day, put Derreck in charge and leave. Pittsburgh was too far from Miami and Vanessa. The sooner he closed the deal, the better.

Victor's was the killer assignment, and he hoped no one would be put in harm's way. Putting together a fight in two weeks was madness, yet he couldn't think of another way to get Roberto "Robbie" Dorado to the states. Hopefully, the kid would insist his mother comes with him.

Nash was unaware if Victor was in contact with his son, and he needed concrete answers. He'd texted the man after he landed in Miami the night before and asked him to come to Gill's today. Nash would offer the job and his grandiose idea.

"Well, Nash? Did you hear me?" Vanessa asked. "Who will take care of Pepita if we're both gone?"

"Missy," Nash answered.

"She hates the bird!" Vanessa laughed. "Remember last time?"

Nash chuckled. "How can I forget? Even though she's not fond of birds, she felt sorry for it and let Pepita out of her cage. It took the whole staff to wrangle up a three-ounce bird. Don't worry, I'll talk to her and probably have to give her a raise, but she'll do it."

Missy had worked with Nash and Vanessa, from the end of the first year they opened until now. Almost ten years older, she came with good business skills and experience, able to take on anything Nash threw at her. He had often left her in charge of the gym. She was his number two after Vanessa, with Nathan as a backup. The four of them were an awesome team, and he hoped it never changed.

"I'm going home early to pack," Vanessa said, stood and stretched.

"Are you doing that on purpose to torture me?"

"Never." She winked and left the room.

"Close the door, please," Nash called after her. He dug for the burner phone in his back pocket to call Mr. Smith.

The last time Nash talked with Mr. Smith, he'd received his assignment at the bunker. His friend, Chase, who'd gotten the short straw and chosen first, had just completed his mission He got to change his last name and go undercover to work for an airline. Nash had to bury his rage when he was given his assignment, help the two men he hadn't chosen to receive the franchise. He'd keep his name. No undercover. No spy games.

"That's it?" Nash had asked Smith incredulously as they finished up in the interrogation room.

"Yes, but there is always more than 'that's it', Mr. Gill," Smith had answered.

Nash had come out of the room swearing and ready to punch a wall at the lame assignment. All he knew was he needed to help Victor and Derreck. Once Smith left the bunker, he was to retrieve a burner phone in an envelope inside the interrogation room. Nash didn't even get to ask Smith if he could call him Charlie, like in Charlie's Angels, to lighten the mood. He'd thought it funny when he'd told Chase, always enjoying a humorous take on things. Chase, not so much. He'd shaken his head wildly and told him to knock it off. "Call him Mr. Smith," he had said.

Mulling over the details, Nash decided to solve both problems and get back to his biggest one, claiming his girl. Yet, after discussing Victor with Vanessa, he knew he was over his head and needed help.

The phone picked up on the second ring.

"Mr. Gill."

"Mr. Smith, I've been doing some thinking, and I need your opinion. What if I arrange a fight between Victor's son and some lightweight right here in Miami? It's the only way I can get Robbie to the states. If there's a better plan, please tell me. I'll offer a big enough purse his people can't resist."

"From the little I know about boxing, isn't a date set months in advance? It involves preparation."

"It's all hype. Gives everyone time to sell tickets, make bets. These fighters are ready. They live in the gym and want to get in the ring."

"I gave you a window of two weeks, but I'm willing to extend if needed."

"Nah, I'm good."

"I have an idea."

"You will help me? Chase said you were a son of a … never mind. Go ahead."

"What if you make it a charity event? The fighters get a set amount, and you donate the rest to Cuban and U.S. charities. Once it's put out there, like in the Twitter Universe, Robbie's people will look foolish if they turn it down."

Nash rubbed the stubble on the side of his face. "I may take you up on the idea and the time. Give me one more week."

"If you need more, call me."

"You are *so* reasonable, Mr. Smith. I'm speechless."

"Don't always believe what you hear, Mr. Gill. Although …"

"Although, what?"

"The more time you take, the others may have to wait, and the window might close on their assignments."

"Shit! I knew it was too good to be true. Stick with your plan, Smith. Change nothing. Is there another Society meeting next Sunday?"

"Yes, but not Sunday. I've scheduled it for Saturday seven p.m."

"I'll be there."

"Are you leaving for Pittsburgh tomorrow?"

"Yeah, how'd you know?" Nash rocked in his chair. "Smith? I said how'd you know? Are you there?" He looked at the phone screen. "Damn! He hung up!"

Nash hopped from his chair and rushed to Vanessa's office. "I got a great idea!" Adrenaline pumped through his body. "We have to start now, before either of us leaves."

"Okay, slow down, big guy." Vanessa pointed to her cell like she'd just gotten off the phone. "C.J. is ready to go. He's psyched. He should be here this afternoon."

"Victor is coming in soon and I'll get him up to speed."

"What's your big idea?"

"A charity event. Think we can pull it off in two weeks' time?"

"Okay, but why the rush? Never mind. I love the idea by the way. We'll have to find a venue, get confirmation from Robbie's camp, let the high rollers and celebrities know it's the place to be seen and a theme. We need a theme!" A frantic look crossed her face. "Let me think on it. While I'm gone, I can still work. Oh, Nash, this is exciting and great marketing for Gill's *and* people will benefit. Make it an annual event."

"Whoa, slow down, Van." Nash grinned. "I'm glad you like it."

"You already give back to the community, make that many communities, but this is a wonderful thing you're doing. Makes me think you've grown up in the short time we've been apart."

"I had a lot of time to think, especially after the guys and I celebrated our birthdays. We turned thirty. Time to do something for the greater good." *I have no idea what I'm doing!*

"Nash!" Missy called up the stairs. "You weren't answering your intercom. You've got a visitor. Should I send him up?"

Nash went to the top of the stairs, smiling at the petite woman with wavy light brown hair, standing with her hands on her hips on the floor below.

"Well?" she asked.

"Is it Victor?"

"The guy you didn't pick for the franchise? I was rooting for him. Poor man escaped with his life from Cuba. He has to share a small bedroom with a teenage nephew in his brother's house."

"Wow, you found out a lot about him."

Missy lifted a shoulder. "What can I say? I'm friendly."

"You are." Nash pointed at her and chuckled. "Send him up."

Nash stayed at the top of the staircase, gazing out over his gym from the railing. Half of the building was second floor while the other had a two-story ceiling giving the gym an open feel. Victor walked on the winding hardwood path leading to the steps. When he looked up, he raised his hand in recognition.

"Nash, I was happy to hear from you." Victor shook hands when he reached the second floor.

"I have a job proposition for you. Come into my office." Nash led the way. "Please, sit."

Once behind his desk, Nash folded his hands on top and studied Victor. *Is he up for the challenge? If not, I need to find another way to help him, and I have no clue what to do.* "I'd like to put you in charge of our boxing room. After our interview, I felt you weren't the right choice for the Charlotte franchise. You'd rather stay here in Miami than move to another state. Am I right?"

"Yes, sir, and thank you for the job offer. I will take it."

"Hold on, you haven't heard everything." Nash held up his hands. "Don't ask me why, but I want to help you get your son and wife to the states."

Victor raised his eyebrows. "You do? Why do you care?"

"Sometimes, people do care, Victor. I heard your story and know your family's at risk even if they don't come here, and you can't return to Cuba."

Victor wiped his face with a hand. "I do not want to go back there to live, and if I did, I'm afraid they will kill me."

"They?"

"Let's say there are people who dislike me."

"Sorry to hear. Are you up for a challenge or not?"

"Yes, whatever you want, I will do it."

"Did you ever hear of the fighter, C. J. Mack?"

"The Mack Attack? If you are in the fight world, as I am, everyone has heard of him. He's an up-and-coming fighter looking for a break. He wants to fight a known name, a winner."

"Like your son?"

Victor's eyes widened. "What are you thinking, Mr. Gill?"

"Please, if we're going to work together, call me Nash."

"Okay … Nash." Victor bobbed his head.

"C.J. is on his way here. You start training him today. I'll take care of the rest."

"How long do I have?"

"Ten days, give or take."

"What?"

"We can do this, Victor. Trust me. Can you get word to your son? Tell him to accept the fight challenge and make sure his mother comes with him to the states."

"I can, yes." Victor tapped the tips of his fingers together and said as if talking to himself, "This might work. Robbie Dorado's papa now trains C.J. Mack. Robbie wants to show he doesn't need me to win, wants to prove he is his own man. That is what I will tell him to say. He must act as if he hates me and is loyal to the …"

"The what?" Nash leaned forward.

"This is very dangerous, Nash. I think you should forget about this. There is a criminal element who edged their way into my business, pushed their own fighters on me, ones who'd throw a fight, so their backers won. They were mere puppets, and I finally could not stomach it anymore. The only boxer they left alone was my son. They saw his potential and his growing popularity. Robbie is a lightweight champ in Cuba. That may be enough for them."

"Then we'll make it sound as if he'll get worldwide exposure, bring in more money for them." Nash cleared his throat. "They'll cash out on illegal betting too, but each man will get a set amount and more for winning. The fight will be part of a charity event with proceeds going to both countries. This criminal element will not look good if they turn it down."

"You almost have me believing it will work, Nash." Victor shook his head. "I hope you are right."

CHAPTER THREE

Vanessa stepped onto the private jet and Andy, a familiar pilot with C.Y. Airlines, greeted her with a handshake. "I see Chase sent his best." She teased.

"Nice to see you again, Vanessa. I hope you have a comfortable flight." Andy looked past her. "And who do we have here? It can't be little Adrian. He was this tall the last time I saw him." He held his hand lower than the boy's height.

"It's me!" The five-year-old jumped up and down.

"And, me!" Rachel, his sister, joined in, hopping from one foot to the other. "I will be in third grade next year."

"You are not." Andy waved a hand. "I thought you were in high school."

"No! I just graduated second grade." Rachel giggled.

Rosa, Vanessa's sister, laughed and nudged her kids into the plane, followed by her husband, Leo. "They grow up too fast. That's what mama says, right, Vanessa?" She stared at her as if shooting daggers.

What did I do now? "Yeah, Rosa, it's what she says."

"Leo, would you mind?" Rosa gave her husband a smile as she looked at their children and stepped around him, linking arms with Vanessa. "I'd like time with my sister."

Oh, no. Here we go.

"Is there something to drink on the flight?" Rosa tapped the attendant in the front before pulling Vanessa farther into the plane.

"Coffee, tea, juice …"

"Let me stop you there," Rosa looked at her watch. "It's still morning but please make us two mimosas."

"Coming right up."

"Thank you."

The sisters settled into two tan leather seats at the back of the small jet. Vanessa waited for the lecture or scolding she was about to receive. Eye rolls and arguments over trivial things, mostly about Vanessa's job, had filled the past two years.

The flight attendant approached and smiled. "Here you go." She set the mimosas on the table between them. The drinks came in two tall glass flutes along with a bag of almonds.

"Thanks," Vanessa said and returned the smile.

"This is the life." Rosa took a sip and put her flute next to Vanessa's. "So nice of Mama to call and invite us, don't you think?"

"Look, Rosa," Vanessa answered, checking her tone. "I can tell you want to say something so out with it."

"Okay," Rosa sat forward and whispered. "What are you thinking? Are you out of your fricking mind? Why would you *ever* break up with Nash Gill? The guy's a billionaire. I have proof! His name is in one of those fancy magazines that lists rich men. Did you fall and hit your head?"

"Really? You think I should stay with Nash because he's rich?"

"Um … yeah." Rosa grinned. "Besides, he's hot, Vanessa! That body, ooh, how can you let another woman touch it? Besides, I love the guy, and you do, too. Come on, I was teasing before. It's all about love, isn't it?"

"New topic." Vanessa folded her arms and stared at her sister.

"We never see you! All you do is work, work and more work. I am happy to get three days with you away from Miami."

"I know, I know. Well, now you vented, I want your help." Vanessa leaned forward and lifted her glass to her lips. "Let's talk Mama into moving back to Miami."

"I don't think she'll come, Van, too many memories." Rosa shook her head. "Since Papi died, it's not the same for her there. Chase did us and her a big favor when he offered her a job. She jumped at the chance to leave Miami."

"He whisked her away to another state. I don't consider it a favor."

"Think about Mama, Van. She's happy at Chase's and we can see her any time. I don't like that she's miles away, either. The kids are far from their grandmother and we can't drop in to see her, but she has a good life. Isn't it what we want for her?" Rosa leaned forward, slyly raising her eyebrows. "But if we found her a man, maybe she'd move back."

Vanessa snickered and let out a breath. "She'd never. You're right. I'd rather have her at Chase's than unhappy in Miami."

* * *

"My girls! My babies!" Renata pulled Rosa and Vanessa into her arms.

"Mama, you act as if you haven't seen us in years," Rosa said with a laugh.

"It was Memorial Day weekend," Vanessa added. "Just a few weeks ago." She felt her phone buzz but ignored it or she'd catch hell from her mom and sister. "Can we settle into our rooms then visit?"

"I have them ready." Renata waved her hand to follow.

Vanessa never got over the beauty of Chase Young's manor. She marveled at its landscape as they rounded a corner to the back of the house. The home had a modern design yet gave off a vibe that royalty lived there. He'd landscaped the grounds making sure everything fit into a natural setting. The family followed a gray stone path past his outdoor living space and pool area to her mom's bungalow.

Chase had built the home to Renata's specifications. Three bedrooms and two baths downstairs with eat-in kitchen and large great room. Two more bedrooms and bath for the grandchildren were on the second floor. *Not really a small bungalow.* Vanessa smiled when they arrived at the home with a Cape Cod feel.

Vanessa knew which bedroom belonged to her and headed down the hall. Renata insisted her daughters choose their décor after designating the color scheme of white and navy with shades of gray as the wall color and the main room's accent. Her mom said to pick any accent color of her choosing. She'd chosen a gray bedframe, navy comforter and pillow shams decorated with large white flowers that reminded her of dandelions when they went to seed. Spring green pillows, sheets and velvet accent chair added the pop of color she liked. She'd placed greenery in forms of potted plants and a silk bamboo tree in strategic spots around the room.

She plopped into the chair and swiped through her phone messages. "I got it!" Vanessa raised her arm in the air. "I have to call Nash." Checking to make sure her door was closed, she dialed his number.

"Van? Are you in Charlotte?" His voice held a touch of concern, making her heart flip.

"Yes, I called to tell you I found the perfect venue and they're holding it for us. You need to get over there, check it out and give them a down payment. If you want more information, I can send you a link to their website."

"I trust you. They'll have the payment in an hour. Text me the address when we're done. Tell me what you envision and why this place works."

"Picture James Bond at Casino Royale."

"I like it."

Everyone is to wear black or white or ... if you dare, orange!"

"Our signature color, I like it. But it's a bright orange."

"It will look cool for a guy's pocket square, tie or bowtie, Nash. Women are inventive. There are many shades of orange right down to peach."

"Hmm, I like peach."

"You're getting off track, big guy."

"Sorry, the scent of you took over for a moment."

"Nash." *Why is he making this so hard?* "I will find the brightest orange dress out there ... designer, of course."

"Put it on my tab."

"I can afford to buy my dress, Nash." Vanessa gripped her top lip with her bottom teeth not wishing to argue. "The place is perfect. A one-story Mediterranean building with rounded arches for entrances. One of the larger dining rooms gives off an orange glow in the picture, and I'm hoping it's really like that. It's beautiful. They even set the tables with orange china. Or we can eat outdoors under a tented canopy with those dangling lightbulbs. Whatever you prefer."

"Indoors. Air conditioning. No bugs."

"Okay. That's settled. We can use another one of their rooms as a casino. Gamble for charity. It will be high end, all crystal, black and white. Plans are to set a black and white dessert table along one wall for the guests to enjoy with a champagne fountain, maybe a chocolate one, too."

"You on my arm would make it perfect, Van."

"I'll be your date if we go as friends."

"Deal!" Nash sounded a little too happy at the prospect.

"Now here's the best part. We can hold the fight outside. Their property goes down to the beach. Picture selling tickets to those who want to see the fight and can't afford to come to the gala. We can have large screens showing the action to beach goers while the high rollers get seating by the ring."

"I'll talk with my security team. Opening it up like that is a great idea but also a major headache."

"Not everyone can afford to come to high society social events, Nash. You've always helped the little *guy*." *Wonder if he noticed I emphasized guy.*

"I like the concept. How soon can you get the invites out?"

"As soon as you tell me. I can work from here. Our social media presence is good, so the word should spread quickly."

A tap came at Vanessa's door. "Van?"

"It's Rosa," Vanessa hissed into the phone, making Nash laugh.

"I'll let you go."

"No, wait." Vanessa turned her head. "I'll be there in a minute, Ro." She lifted her phone to her ear. "Did C.J. show up?"

"With an entourage." Nash chuckled. "They're good guys."

"I thought you were leaving today?"

"I wanted to wait for C.J. to arrive. Now that he's here and working with Victor, I'll send Andy a text I'm ready to leave."

"He flew back to Miami for you?"

"Yeah, and he said the strangest thing. Chase showed up at C.Y. in a blue Honda. I didn't think he'd be caught dead in anything but his Aston Martin."

"Times are a changing." Vanessa giggled. "I'll see you on Thursday … or whenever you get back."

"Vanessa! I'm not dumb. You're working in there." Rosa's voice came through the door. "I won't tell Mama if you let me in."

"Fine." Vanessa strolled to the door and leaned on the edge when she opened it. "See? I'm not doing anything."

Rosa stepped in the room and glanced around. "You haven't unpacked. Your luggage is right where the staff left it."

"I was resting."

Rosa walked to the bed and sat on the edge. "Van, what's happened to us? We used to be the best of friends. Remember when we were little, we had our own secret club. One look or nod sent us flying to our bedroom for a meeting."

Vanessa laughed. "I do, and I think we're having one now."

"We are?" Rosa smiled. "Tell me what's going on."

"If I do, promise you won't tell Mama when I'm working on my phone."

Rosa placed her hand over her heart. "I swear on my children's precious heads."

Vanessa confided how she had ten days to pull off a high society charity event for Nash.

"Why so sudden?"

Vanessa lifted a shoulder. "You know him. He gets an idea and wants it finished yesterday. We're backing a new fighter, something he's never done before. He hired Victor Dorado to run the boxing room. Maybe he wants to introduce him to the public as Gill's world class trainer."

"Dorado? Why does the name sound familiar?"

"Three years ago, he escaped from Cuba. His story was out there for a while, but now he lives a quiet life with his brother. He dreams of bringing his wife and son to the states." Vanessa paused. "Wait a minute." She stared at her sister. "You don't think Nash is helping him? He wants C.J. to fight Robbie Dorado."

Rosa's eyes widened. "I think you're right, and it sounds a little dangerous. I'm in."

"What?"

"I want to help, Van. I'll volunteer. Adrian and Rachel are in summer camp for the rest of the month. It will be like they're in school. I have free time on my hands."

"What about all the lectures you gave me on how great it is to be home with the kids?" Vanessa closed one eye.

"It is. But I don't want to forget about me. I thought when Adrian started Kindergarten in August, I'd look for a part-time job," Rosa said. "Nash is too kind and keeps paying the kids' tuition. I got a notice from the school the bills are paid for the upcoming school year."

"Nash is fully aware you like that private school, Ro. When he makes a pledge, he honors it. Were you worried he wouldn't pay since we broke up?"

"Maybe."

"That's why you were thinking about getting a job." Vanessa folded her arms over her chest. "What if you come to Gill's and work there once the kids start school? Flexible hours."

"Really?" Rosa pulled Vanessa down on the bed next to her. "I miss this. The two of us planning things together. Thanks."

"You're … welcome?" Vanessa wrinkled her brow. "You don't have to thank me. I wish you'd told me sooner."

"We've been oil and water for a while, Van. I don't know how it started, but let's not let it happen again. Deal?"

Vanessa wrapped her arm around her sister's shoulders. "Deal."

"Now, before we get too deep into decorations, finding the right gambling tables, dealers and hosts, I want to talk about Robbie Dorado. There's talk in the community he's under the influence of a corrupt organization in Cuba. It sounds dangerous. Is Nash aware?"

"I'm sure he is." Vanessa rubbed her chin. "Wait a minute. There's more to this than a charity event. If Robbie's camp accepts the challenge, they'd be in Miami for a few days. Victor could easily help his son disappear after the fight."

"What about the wife?"

"She's part of the deal, I'm sure. Robbie wouldn't come without her."

"Van, Nash isn't stupid. If we figured it out, I'm sure Robbie's handlers will, too."

"He must have a plan." Vanessa shook her head. "Right now, we need to put it aside and focus on getting everything coordinated. Let's start with the menu and make sure they serve only quality wine and liquor. After they eat dinner, the guests will move into the casino. We need ideas for black and white dessert ideas, even if we have to ship them in."

"I'll get on it."

"We can do the menu and decor together. I'll work on making Casino Royale a top-notch destination transforming people to another place as they walk through the doors." Vanessa stared out at the pool, listening to the water splash from the rocks to the surface below. "Like this place makes you feel."

"What about invites?"

"I plan to work on them here by the pool. Can you distract Mama if she gets too close?"

"Yes." Rosa rubbed her hands together. "Leo and Mama get the kids and I can help you. Leo said I deserved time to myself."

"He's such a good husband, Rosa. You're lucky he puts up with you." Vanessa teased.

Rosa nudged her and they laughed. "Remember when we dated? You said to snap him up, and I did." She turned to Vanessa with a serious look. "Now, sister, you need to do the same."

"Nash never asked me to marry him, Ro." Vanessa hung her head. "A year ago, I'd have said yes in a heartbeat. Now? Watching him award another franchise to a man has changed me. Women deserve an equal chance. They make it to the short list but never the finals."

"Hey, he doesn't see it like that. He hires minorities all the time."

"Men," Vanessa huffed.

"I have an idea." Rosa held up her pointer finger. "What if you don't show up to work for a few days? Let him see what it's like without you there. Nash has no clue how much you do and how you keep the place running."

"When this is over, I may try it." Vanessa looked over at her luggage. "I guess I should unpack, find my bathing suit and meet you by the pool."

"Early dinner on the patio." Rosa rubbed her stomach. "Although I'm starving now."

"If I know Mama, she'll have plenty of appetizers and snacks by the pool. See you out there?"

"Yeah," Rosa said as she slid off the bed. "Thanks again, little sis, for the talk. I'm happy we're a team again."

"So am I."

CHAPTER FOUR

"I need a plan," Nash grumbled as he paced his office. "What have I gotten into?" He ran his hand over the stubble on his face. "Luckily, Vanessa's on top of things as usual. Oh!" He picked up the office phone and hit the intercom button. "Missy?"

"Yeah, boss?"

"I'm going to cut a check and have you deliver it to the venue for our charity event."

"I wasn't aware we had a charity event planned."

"We do."

"So, now I know. I'll be right up."

When Missy appeared at the door, she smiled and shook her head. "Is Vanessa working on this?"

"From Chase's." He nodded. "She's already got things moving. I'm sure you'll hear from her."

Missy held up her phone. "Already on our Facebook page." She studied the screen. "I like it. People will flock to the beach for the fight. Will they have access to food and drink?"

"I never thought that far ahead. Could you text Vanessa and ask? I have to get to the airport."

"Pennsylvania, right?" Missy lifted a brow. "Another guy I liked for the job lives there. Derreck Mills."

"How did you know he was from P.A.?" Nash waved his hand. "Never mind. You two talked."

"He hoped you'd want to build a gym in Pittsburgh and keep him in mind. I didn't have the heart to tell him you never would."

"Logistics."

"Right, so why are you going?"

"I want to help him."

"Another charity event?"

"Missy, you ask too many questions." Nash glanced around his office. "I thought I brought a bag to work."

"Your carry on?" Missy asked and said without waiting for a response. "You left it in the front office downstairs."

"Thanks. I hope to see you back here on Thursday."

"Same day Vanessa returns." Missy turned to leave and hesitated. She spun on her heels and said, "You two are good together, Nash."

"Then why did she …?" He looked at his friend with questioning eyes.

"See her the way she wants to be seen. Once you do, you'll be back together. She didn't want to break up with you. I see it in her eyes every time she looks at you. Good luck on your trip and tell Derreck I said hi. I guess I'll be on Pepita duty while you're gone." Missy rolled her eyes.

"Hey, you forgot something," Nash said, holding out the check. "Thanks for doing this, Missy. I'd go myself but don't have time. Check the place out if you want while you're there. And don't pay for tickets. You and Nathan are comped."

"Thanks, I'll tell my husband." She winked.

"Vanessa will want you to wear an orange dress, but that's where my expertise ends. You'll need to get together with her."

"Also comped?" Missy teased.

"Yes, I'm paying for everything. Don't fight me on it. Tell Nathan the same thing … and don't let the bird out of the cage this time." He winked.

Missy took the check and left the office as his phone gave off a ping. Nash checked, seeing Andy's name on the screen. He'd landed in Miami and was ready to go anytime.

Nash rushed down the stairs, grabbed his luggage and headed out to his Ferrari. From the original Gill's Gym, the airport was a half hour drive from Miami Beach. He picked up speed on the highway and soon pulled into a parking spot by the terminals for private jets. He jogged to the waiting area, wishing he could share his assignment with someone but knew he had to keep it a secret. He'd have to keep up the pretense it was strictly a charity event but even with his mission hanging over his head, Nash looked forward to the actual day. *I can't stand it! Vanessa picked a James Bond theme. That's my girl!*

Nash found Andy in the waiting area, made small talk and followed him to the plane.

"Do you have a rental car?" Andy asked. "I can arrange one for you."

"Thanks, but I already called for one. Sorry you're flying all over the country today, Andy. this is later than I first said, but I had to finish up some business."

Nash had stayed at the gym to wait for the fighter, C.J. Mack. He didn't want to leave before meeting him plus he wanted to check the guy out. Vanessa said his fighting weight fell into the lightweight class but if it didn't, he'd need to scramble to find someone else to get in the ring with Robbie. The man had walked in with an entourage and Nash was uncertain if Victor would like it. Nash wasn't too fond of four guys hanging around the gym, but when he'd met them, he changed his mind. One turned out to be C.J.'s sparring partner, one kept the fighter's appointments, another was his best friend, and the last was the driver.

Andy broke into Nash's thoughts and said, "I flew in and out of Charlotte today and even talked with the boss when he stopped by. Flight classes don't begin until Monday, so I'll enjoy my time in the air."

Nash liked when he had the plane to himself although he enjoyed company and joking with friends. He didn't feel up to it today. He couldn't help thinking about Vanessa in an orange dress, halter top and slit up to the top of her thigh, her mahogany eyes beckoning to him. When they landed, he'd browse a few sites and look for designer dresses. "Or I could have it made specially for her. She'd see how much I care. Damn! Why didn't I think of this before?" He ran his hand through his waves, making sure his hair was in place. "I'll call Kade when I land. Got to invite the boys to the party anyway."

The Society used to call Kade Phillips "Tiger Eyes" in college. His amber eyes and mysterious good looks, shaggy haircut and lean, muscular figure were the perfect characteristics for a male model. He did a few gigs to earn money during and after college but never wanted it as a career. Instead, he wished to be on the other side of the camera, started off doing photo shoots and worked his way through the industry. He now owned a piece of a film studio and a few other holdings, even directed a movie and a few shows for cable. With Chase's help, he'd invested his money wisely.

Nash suddenly recalled a conversation from last Sunday. Kade wanted to back a new designer and get into the fashion industry. Vanessa would like he was helping a newcomer and would love to showcase their dress. He'd put Missy in touch with Kade, too, and they could work on ideas. "I am the mastermind, if I say so myself." Nash smiled.

"Nash?" Andy's voice came over the intercom. "We'll land in fifteen."

The two flight attendants, who'd flown many times with him, had left Nash alone during the flight. They'd seemed to realize he needed space. He'd usually ask them to sit down and quizzed them on their families and lives, making jokes along the way. Not today. His mind was focused on what lay ahead of him.

The landing went smoothly, and Nash found the rental he'd ordered, a full-size of whatever they had available. He found the keys inside and set his GPS. Having never been in Pittsburgh, he hoped the hotel was decent and the restaurant Derreck had chosen served good food. Nash rubbed his eyes as he headed downtown. "I'm never tired. It must be this 'weight of the world' feeling I've got. Damn! I hope I don't age five years like Chase did." He chuckled thinking back to seeing his friend at the end of his first week of assignment, tired and drawn.

"Call Kade," Nash told his phone and waited for his friend to answer.

"Nash, buddy! I didn't think I'd hear from you so soon. What's up?"

"I need your help."

"Okay, fire away."

"Two designer dresses before next Saturday."

"I'm on it."

Not surprised by his response, Nash recited part of their mantra. "From the bottom to the top, right?"

"You got it."

Over the years, each member tested the Society's pledge and the guys always came through no matter the request. "Vanessa and Missy will contact you. But Van's dress needs to be Gill's Gym orange, Kade … and sexy. Try to talk her into a slit up the leg to the top of her thigh."

"She's got the legs for it."

"You look at her legs?" Nash yelled. "When I see you on Saturday, you better start running."

Kade laughed. "You won't have your dresses if you kill me."

"I won't kill you, just leave you with a warning."

"Fine, but you know we look at each other's women, Nash. Van's been part of us for five years. How can we not notice how fine she is?"

"You won't be hanging out with her again. We're not together."

"Again?"

"She broke up with me after I gave the new franchise in Charlotte to a great guy, an army vet."

"Oh."

"You say 'oh' like you know something. Out with it."

"Nope, I know nothing," Kade answered. "But, if I know Vanessa, she'd like a chance at a franchise."

"I can't live without her. She stays at Gill's with me, together or not."

"You're holding her prisoner?" Kade chuckled, then clicked his tongue. "And she doesn't have a clue. Is that why you've ignored her pleas for her own gym these past two years?"

"No … maybe! Hey, we've gotten off course here. Missy can have any shade of orange she wants, but I'd prefer she chose ours."

"They'll both have great dresses, Nash. Is the Society invited?"

"Of course. I plan to tell them Saturday, but everyone should get a formal invite in the mail and a cool-looking email, plus it's all over social media."

"This is a Smith thing, right?"

"Yeah, and pray it works. It's the only idea I got."

"Can you tell me what the plan is?"

"No, but once you get all the details, hopefully you'll figure it out. I may need you guys, Kade, to complete this damn assignment. When your turn comes, I'll tell you one thing in advance, Smith is no help."

"Maybe my turn won't come. We'll find out if Chase completed his mission this weekend. If he didn't, we better apply for jobs."

"Smith must have faith in us. He gave me my assignment before Chase finished his," Nash answered.

"True, it's a good sign."

"Are you in New York City or Denver, Kade?"

"NYC. Setting up shop for my new designer. Jordan's first collection will come out next spring."

"Good luck with your new venture. I'll let you go. See you Saturday." Nash hung up as he pulled into his hotel and waited for a valet. "Hello, Pittsburgh."

* * *

"I'll pick you up tomorrow and drive you out to my high school, Nash." Derreck, once a quarterback for his school's team and now a coach at his alma mater, ran his hand over his closely cropped black hair. "I want you to see everything first-hand. The kids are so dedicated, they come to work outs before the practice season starts."

Derreck had insisted on picking up the dinner tab so Nash refrained from ordering another beer. "I can feel your passion," he said. "I'm looking forward to seeing the school."

"Can I be blunt?" Derreck asked.

"Sure."

"Why are you here? You didn't choose me for the franchise and Missy told me you'd never build a gym in Pittsburgh."

"Right, on both accounts. But you really didn't want the franchise, did you?" Nash stared at him.

"No, I was hoping you'd see the need for one here."

"Can I be blunt?" Nash asked.

"Of course."

"Once I see the high school and surrounding land, you may get your gym. Not a Gill's, but a gym."

"What?" Derreck's eyes widened in surprise. "Did I hear you right?"

"Everything I do is not about money," Nash said in a low voice. "I saw something in you, Derreck. You want to help these kids better their lives. The world needs more Derreck Mills' in it, but also, they need someone to back them. You have the passion. I have the money."

"We talk about that in the teachers' lounge every so often." Derreck chuckled. "If only we had a few rich backers, imagine what we could do in the education field."

Nash held out his hands. "Here I am. Impress me."

"I'll pick you up out front of your hotel at nine a.m."

* * *

Every woman with long dark hair caught Nash's attention while he waited for Derreck's arrival. He knew they weren't Vanessa but hoped they were, daydreaming she couldn't stay away and had come looking for him in Pittsburgh. An image of her running into his arms felt so real, he almost missed Derreck pulling up to the curb.

Nash hopped in the passenger side as Derreck held up a fast food bag. "Did you have breakfast? I've got a couple of egg and bacon sandwiches in here. I remembered you don't drink coffee, so I got you bottled water."

"Thanks." Nash took the bag and peeked inside with a smile. "Haven't had one of these in a while."

"Help yourself and throw me one."

Fifteen minutes later, they pulled into the school's parking lot. Derreck steered the car around back and said, "Closer to the gym."

Three young men leaned against the brick wall by the metal door.

"It's about time you got here, Coach," one said, lifting a side of his mouth.

"Who do we have here?" another asked. "You look like you could audition for my position. Offense or defense?"

"Guys, stand down," Derreck said in a quiet tone. The teens smiled and nodded yet followed directions. "This is Nash Gill of Gill's Gyms. He's here to watch you work out."

"Mr. Gill." One of the teens stepped forward and extended his hand. "Nice to meet you." The other two did the same.

Once inside, the young men ignored Nash and went about their business.

"It's hot in here," Nash said to Derreck. "When will the air kick in?"

"We don't have air conditioning. This is as good as it gets. We take a lot of breaks and drink plenty of water."

Nash glanced at the guys working with weights and running laps. "What else you got?"

"Not much. We make do."

Nash studied the walls and floors of the old building, clean yet rundown, but in dire need of help. "Why don't I start here first? New gym with workout room." He wiped sweat forming on his brow. "And air conditioning."

"For the whole school?" Derreck looked at him from the corner of his eye. "Don't want the general population to hate the football team, except when they have P.E."

"Sure, I can do it." In his head, Nash made a list of things to accomplish in Pittsburgh and became overwhelmed. *Where do I get the money? Smith says we can't use ours.* A brilliant thought came to him. "In fact, I'm having a charity event a week from Saturday. Your school will go on the list of places we will help."

"It will help the kids at this school, Nash. I appreciate it." Derreck looked away as if he was watching his guys workout.

"But?"

Derreck turned his head to face Nash. "My dream is a place for all kids to go after school, a study area, computer room and gym. A community center for the neighborhood."

"That's a tall order."

"I'm asking a lot." Derreck shook his head.

"Can you teach, coach and run a fitness center?" Nash highly doubted the man had the time and energy to fully commit.

"Yes."

"You seem pretty sure of yourself." Nash chuckled. "Where would you want it built?"

"There's property for sale less than a five-minute walk from here. I did my research and it doesn't need rezoning. While kids are in school, it would be open to the community. I'd set a stipend for use of the facility and if people can't afford it, come anyway and offer your help. I'm hoping to get volunteers and a few paid workers to run it during that time. As soon the neighborhood schools are dismissed, the center becomes a place for kids. I have quite a few teachers willing to help with homework, using the computers and working with the kids in the gym."

"And your football team?"

"Hopefully, they'd get a special room." Derreck winked.

Nash realized his simple plan of building a gym and leaving it in Derreck's hands would not work out. He couldn't fund it yet, and even if he sent a crew, they'd want to be paid. "Tell you what. Give me six weeks, and I'll have an answer for you. The school is a definite go and will be part of the charity event, but the other will take time."

Derreck shook Nash's hand. "It's all I can ask for."

"Would you mind driving me back to the hotel? I need to catch up on some work."

"Of course." Derreck's face said it all. He was thrilled he didn't need to sell his idea to Nash. "If you don't mind, I'd like to drive you past the property on the way."

When the car pulled up in front of the hotel, Nash looked at Derreck and smiled. "You've done your homework. I like the location of the land. It will need some clean-up before any excavation starts but I'm getting ahead of myself. First, we need to buy the property. We'll keep in touch. Hope you have a winning season."

"Thanks, Nash."

Nash watched the car pull away and searched for the burner phone in his pocket. Once inside his room, he pressed the one button that would connect him to Smith.

"Hello, Mr. Gill. How's the weather in Pittsburgh?"

"Hot," Nash growled. "Let's cut the small talk and get to the reason I'm calling. There's a piece of property I want to buy, or should I say, you need to buy. I don't want to lose out waiting for you to return my money."

Smith rattled off the address. "Is that the property?"

"You already have the address?" Nash waited for a response but got none.

Mr. Smith continued, "The venue for the charity event is perfect. I have to admit, I didn't think you'd complete your other task as quickly as this one."

"I got Vanessa on the job. She takes no prisoners."

"Your ex. Very capable woman."

"What? Have you met her?"

"I did not say I did, Mr. Gill. Women are as good at their jobs as men."

"Not you, too!" Nash exclaimed. "Look, Smith, stay out of my personal business. I'm aware Van can run one of my franchises with one hand tied behind her back. I just ..."

"You wouldn't lose her," Smith said softly.

"Are you spying on me or reading my mind?" Nash shouted. "Look, do as I ask. Buy the property and save it for me, will you?" He paused. "Smith? Did you hear me?"

Nash stared at the phone, shaking his head. "He hung up … again." He dashed off a text to Vanessa to say he'd talked to Kade. "He'll hook you up with whatever you want," he told her. She hadn't responded to any of his messages, but he hoped she would soon.

CHAPTER FIVE

Vanessa planned to spend her day poolside. Her niece and nephew came and went with their dad, but Rosa stayed with her. "I got a text from Nash," Vanessa told Rosa. "He said to contact Kade for my dress. I better tell him you'll be working for us until the charity event."

"Kade?" Rosa took off her sunglasses and put one end of a temple in her mouth. "He's the yummy one, the model. I have a hard time remembering who's who when it comes to Nash's friends. They're all hot, but each one has something the others don't."

"Rosa!"

"I'm allowed to look." She winked.

"And Kade's not a model … well, he was at one time."

"I still have the ads he was in saved to a folder on my computer. I like to look at them every once in a while." She gave Vanessa a Cheshire cat smile.

"Let's get off the subject of you and hot men." Vanessa looked down at her phone. "I just heard back from Nash. He said to thank you for helping and, of course, you deserve a dress."

"Yes!" Rosa pumped her arm in the air. "Do you want to get started? Send Kade a message and see what he says."

"If I remember, he's getting into the fashion business and backing a new designer. He'll probably want us to wear him or her."

"Did Kade give you the designer's name?"

"No." Vanessa typed a quick message. "But, if Kade's interested, the designer's good."

"It's fine with me. I've got no complaints."

"Oh! He answered me already. He says he was waiting for my text and has pulled together some color choices, and Jordan is working on sketches."

"Jordan? We still don't know if it's a him or her. What do you think?"

"Woman," Vanessa answered and paused. "If I know Nash, we're wearing orange. I definitely want to wear bright orange to represent Gill's."

"It will look good with your olive skin and dark hair, Van. Me? What do you think?"

"A dark peach." Rosa was fairer than Vanessa but still had dark hair, cut to her shoulders.

"I like it."

"I'll tell Kade to keep it simple. I wonder how fast Jordan can make three dresses?"

"Three?"

"Missy, too."

"What about Mama?"

"She'd never go for a designer dress." Vanessa lifted her sunglasses and peeked under them. "Do you think she will come?"

"I'm sure Chase can talk her into it if she says no to us." Rosa reached for the iced tea pitcher. "I can't see why she wouldn't come. Who could pass up a high society gala?"

"There's going to be a gala?" Renata approached them with a tray of sandwiches.

"Yes, Mama, and you're invited." Vanessa took the platter and placed it on a table between her and Rosa. Renata would never agree to have a dress made for her, so she said, "How about if we three girls go shopping after dinner, Mama? We'll help you look for a dress."

"I'm sure I have something in my closet."

"Mama," Rosa said. "Is it couture?"

"No, Rosa, I buy my dresses from retail stores."

"Do you have an appropriate white, black or orange formal dress, long or short?" Vanessa asked.

"Well … no." Renata raised her hands. "Okay, take me shopping."

"It will be fun, Mama." Vanessa extended her arm and took her mother's hand. "So, that means you'll come to Miami?"

"I wouldn't miss seeing my daughters dressed up for a ball now, would I?"

"It's not a fairytale," Rosa said. "We're hosting a charity event."

"We?" Renata turned to Rosa.

"I'm hired by Gill's until then."

"I thought you two were up to something." Renata laughed. "I am happy to see my daughters working together. When I see him, I will thank Nash for bringing you back to each other."

Guilt swept through Vanessa. *She knew Rosa and I weren't getting along?* "We're fine, Mama, and always have been. I got busy with work and Rosa with her kids."

"If you say so." Renata lifted a shoulder. "I'll change into my swimsuit and join you."

"Really?" Vanessa asked, surprised by her mom's statement.

"I only go in when no one is around," Renata said in a stage whisper. "Have to keep up a professional appearance when Chase and the boys are around."

Rosa looked at Vanessa, and they began to laugh. "Oh, Mama!" they said together.

* * * *

Thursday morning, a car took Vanessa to C.Y. Airlines. Her sister's family would stay until Saturday and Rosa begged her to extend her visit yet knew she had much to do. Vanessa hoped she'd run into Chase at the airline, but his receptionist said he'd been there Tuesday and she hadn't seen him since.

Vanessa arrived at the waiting area, and her phone rang. "Beau?" She answered as she pulled the door open and found a seat in the comfortable space. Andy, the pilot, was busy at the counter but she didn't mind as it gave her time to talk.

"Hey, Van. My schedule opened and I flew in today. Can we meet for dinner?"

"Sure. I'll check in at the office, drop my stuff at home and change. How does seven sound?"

"Perfect. I'm picking up my rental as we speak. I'll drive to Nash's and will meet you at his favorite oceanfront restaurant."

"I can't wait to see you and catch up … and I may need your help with the charity event."

"I got the invite. Well done, even without my help."

"No suggestions or corrections?" Vanessa teased, wondering if he was serious or joking. Sometimes it was hard to tell with Beau.

"It looks great," Beau answered. "Isn't Nash supposed to come home today?"

"I think so. He never gave me a time."

"Maybe I'll see him at the house. I need to talk to him, too. See you later?"

"Yes," Vanessa said and ended the call. "Oh, Nash, you're such a good guy. You even have rooms for your friends in your home."

Nash had built an oceanfront compound with pool, dock and yacht included. Plush landscaping made a person feel like they were at a private tropical island. The sprawling ranch home had a wing for visitors and friends while the rest was fashioned to Nash's needs.

Andy waved from the counter. "Vanessa? Any time you'd like to leave, the plane is ready."

"Now is fine, Andy." Vanessa collected her belongings and followed him outside. "It doesn't seem right for you to fly one person to Miami."

Andy smiled. "That's what a private airline does, Vanessa. We give great service and hope you keep using C.Y. See why?"

Vanessa stifled a laugh. "Yes, I do. I'll always use this airline. Chase would kill me if I didn't."

Andy tipped his flight cap. "Right, you are."

The plane took off within ten minutes of boarding. Vanessa made it home by mid-afternoon, giving her time to stop by the gym.

"Thank goodness, you're back!" Missy ran from the glass-enclosed front office and hugged Vanessa. "For such a small bird, she makes a lot of noise."

"Pepita?" Vanessa wrinkled her brow. "She's pretty quiet or I wouldn't have her in my office."

"Yes, who else would I be talking about?" Missy's light brown wavy hair was pulled into a high ponytail. It swung back and forth with every gesture she made. "We heard the little thing all the way down here." She lifted a shoulder. "I admit I have her on speaker to make sure she stayed alive until you got back, so she probably heard everything going on down here."

"You may be right. She's usually not noisy." Vanessa cocked her head. "I don't hear her now."

"She knows you're back, I guess, probably heard your voice. I'm on the two-way intercom so I can talk to her." Missy dropped her shoulders. "Stressful. That's all I can say."

"You better never get a pet, Missy." Vanessa laughed.

"Nathan said the same thing." Missy chuckled. "Two kids keep us busy enough with sports and dance. Did I tell you Mason wants to start boxing lessons?"

"Isn't he too young?"

"Mason is fourteen, going to be fifteen soon, Van."

"What? I still picture him as a nine-year-old kid. Dare I ask how old Lexie is?"

"Twelve. My babies aren't so little anymore."

Vanessa rubbed Missy's forearm. "I'll check on my baby now." She closed one eye. "And she better be alive." She couldn't stay serious and laughed.

"She is! Trust me!" Missy called after her.

Vanessa jogged up the stairs and into her office. Pepita, alive and well, scooted to her corner for a treat. "Hello, baby girl. How's my little Pita?" The bird chirped before taking a nut from Vanessa. "Your favorite, a sliver of almond."

Her desk looked untouched except for a pile of messages. Vanessa checked her office phone for the same. "Nothing that can't wait. Whoa! Wait a minute!" She buzzed Missy.

"Hello."

"Is Victor here?"

"In the back. Want me to get him?"

"If you would, thanks. I'm in my office."

"Is Greenie still breathing?"

Greenie? Aww, she loves Pepita. "Yes, she's fine."

Vanessa shuffled through some 'while you were away' notes and logged onto her computer. One email stood out when she got to her work account.

"You wanted to see me?" Victor stood in the doorway.

"Yes, please, come in and sit down." Vanessa leaned back and folded her arms over her chest. "It doesn't take a genius to figure out what you and Nash are up to." She inhaled and let out a slow breath. "Let me rephrase it … what Nash is doing. He dreamed up this whole fight and charity event to get your family to the states. How dangerous is this?" She'd watched Victor's eyebrows rise into his forehead as she spoke. She knew she was right.

Victor cleared his throat. "It should not be dangerous if everything goes according to plan. I have been in touch with my people in Cuba and spoken to Robbie. From what he told me, my people have given him helpful instructions. He must be a good actor and pretend to hate me. Robbie will insist on fighting to show his traitorous father he is still a champion without him."

"If these men," Vanessa made quotes with her fingers. "Who are in control now trust him, then it will go well. If they see it as I do, there could be big trouble."

"I will take full responsibility." Victor dropped his head. "I am forever grateful to Nash for even attempting to try this."

"Well, I called you in here to tell you they've accepted the challenge. I have a voicemail and email confirmation. And thank goodness they did. I've sent invitations and been spreading the news since Tuesday." Vanessa rubbed her chin. "Although I think I could've found someone to fight C.J. if Robbie's camp declined."

Victor lifted his head, eyes wide. "They accepted?"

"Yes, with stipulations. I got an attachment with the email. We'll go over their demands when Nash gets back." Vanessa looked at the door. "He isn't back yet, is he?"

"No, he's not. I wanted to tell him C.J. is a good choice to fight my son. I wanted to congratulate him on a job well done."

"No need. You're looking at the person who brought in C.J."

"Oh! Well, then, thank *you*." Victor bobbed his head. "If there isn't anything else, I'd like to get back to work."

"We're finished for now. The next eight days will be crazy, Victor. I hope we get a good outcome for you and your family."

* * *

After arriving home, Vanessa threw her gym clothes and travel wear into her laundry basket and headed for the bathroom. From her Miami Beach apartment, it would be a ten-minute ride to the restaurant, so she had time to spoil herself with a long shower.

The scent of peaches soon filled the air and Vanessa drifted to another place as the water soothed her travel weary body. She envisioned a tropical paradise, one so familiar she felt as if she'd been transported there. Nash climbed out of his pool, dripping wet, and shook his body to remove the excess liquid. She watched him move in slow motion toward her, flinging his hair back as water droplets formed a halo around him. The muscles on his arms tightened as he grew closer, and the tattoo running down his bicep made her shiver with pleasure. Soon she'd be in his arms, feeling loved and protected. His lips landing on hers the second he was close enough, and "I love you" said with such sincerity it would make her heart ache.

"Damn!" Vanessa slapped the shower wall. "Stop!"

Her sister's parting words came to her. "Do you want another woman touching him, Van? Kissing him, making love to him instead of you?" Rosa had stared at her for a long minute. "Really think about what you're doing. But, if you're determined to make him see what it's like without you in his life, remember what I said. Disappear for a few days. Don't show up for work. He won't be able to stand it. Just don't do it for *too* long."

"Good advice, Sis." Vanessa pulled a towel from its spot and wrapped it around her body. Once dry she dropped the towel to the floor and studied her figure. She'd been given a Goddess body as her mother liked to call it. Large breasts and back end, yet she'd never be a svelte model.

"If you dieted down to your hip bones, you'd be a size six, Vanessa. You're not a tiny girl," her mama would say when she complained as a teen everyone else was a size zero. "Be grateful for the body you have. Most women would kill for it." She'd wink and say, "Besides, you got that figure from me."

Vanessa tossed a berry-color sundress with a trail of blue and white flowers scattered along the hemline over her head. The deep rounded neckline showed off her best feature. She loved the casual feel of the dress and double-checked the front and back before slipping on sandals and heading out the door to her red mustang, a present from Nash. She debated if she wanted to put the white top down. "What the heck!" She lowered it then pulled away from the apartment.

As she drove, the wind blowing through her hair made her feel free, and the ride gave her time to think. *Beau will help me sort this out. He's known Nash for over ten years. Who else better?*

Vanessa turned into the restaurant's parking lot, tossed the keys to the valet with a ten-dollar bill and spotted Beau on the veranda waiting for her. "Beau!" She raised her hand in greeting.

Her sister, Rosa had been right about one thing. All of Nash's friends were hot. Most had facial hair, and Beau was no exception with a few days' growth of mustache and beard which traveled along his lip and jawline. He looked cool and casual in a pale blue cotton shirt and gray shorts. His coffee-colored eyes connected with hers as she approached. He was two inches taller than Nash, topping out at six feet three and she stood on tiptoe to kiss his cheek. "Hi."

"Hi, yourself. You look rested, Vacation did you good," Beau answered. "Want to sit on the deck or inside?"

"Out. It's always cooler by the ocean." Vanessa nudged him. "You'll get used to the heat."

"It takes a while." Beau laughed and turned to the hostess. "Two for the deck, please."

The hostess glanced at Vanessa. "Isn't Nash coming?"

"Not today."

"Well," she said and looked at Beau. "If you're going to be in town for the weekend, I'm available." She walked through the restaurant and out to the deck, swaying her hips. "How's this?" The hostess asked Beau with a rehearsed lip pout never looking in Vanessa's direction.

"Fine, thank you."

As Vanessa slipped by the hostess, she whispered, "You couldn't handle him." And gave her a sweet smile.

"You know everyone here, don't you?" Beau asked pulling his chair closer to the table.

"Most of the staff, yeah. She's…" Vanessa lifted her chin in the hostess' direction. "New. Been around a few months. I swear she hits on everyone. Oh! No offense." Vanessa wasn't sure if it was true, but no twenty-one-year old was going to sink her claws into Beau.

"None taken." Beau smiled. "Besides, she's a little young."

"Oh, I forgot! Aren't you going out with Bett or…?" Vanessa wrinkled her brow.

"Bethany? No."

Vanessa gave him a sad look. "Sorry to hear. I thought you two were getting serious."

The waiter interrupted their conversation, and they ordered drinks and dinner at the same time. Vanessa waited until the server walked away from the table. "Tell me about Bethany. What happened? You were serious, right?"

"Until she became aware of my working-class upbringing." He smirked.

"What?" Vanessa leaned over the table and said in a low voice, "You're a billionaire. What's not to like?"

"Bethany grew up with money. It didn't matter how much I had, a million or a billion. Appearances? Well, that was a different story. She liked I went to Harvard, took her to exclusive restaurants, front row seats for events and even had wealthy friends. I didn't talk much about family, just in passing, until Mama insisted I bring her home. After a year of dating, she thought it was time."

"And you took her to Brooklyn."

"Yes, despite my efforts to buy mom and dad a new house, they won't move. Mama said they saved and bought their home with hard-earned money and were staying. She'll take my money for renovations and new furniture but that's all. Bethany took one look around the neighborhood and I knew she wasn't impressed." Beau smiled. "I realized right then as we entered my parents' living room, she wasn't the right girl for me. She acted polite yet aloof."

"I really don't like her now." Vanessa made a face. "I love your parents! They're warm and welcoming. The upgrades to the house are awesome. You're a good son, Beau."

Drinks came and Vanessa held up her glass. "To your parents."

"I'll second that." Beau reached for his Manhattan, his go-to drink.

Vanessa admired how even kneeled he was, especially with the friends he had. Beau was good for Nash and the only one who made him see when he headed down the wrong path. But Beau credited Nash for keeping him real and less serious than he could be.

"My parents had asked me to help my younger brothers instead of them. They wanted them to get a good start in life. They said they didn't need much and were happy. I'd love to give them more but what can I do?" Beau leaned back as the server placed his dinner on the table.

"Oldest child syndrome, you're the over-achiever." Vanessa sipped her drink. "Your brothers? One's in college and the other is three years younger than you?" She looked up at the server. "Thanks."

"My youngest brother Brandon's at UConn doing his thing. He just finished his freshman year."

Vanessa wrinkled her brow. "Refresh my memory. I have a tough time keeping track of Nash's friends, let alone their siblings."

"Brandon got a basketball scholarship to the University of Connecticut. He'll start his second year this fall. He keeps his grades up yet he's dedicated to basketball. Blake went to Boston College and got a business degree. He wanted to work for me and now he does."

"Right, at your tech company, the security branch." Vanessa shook her hair back from her face. "Now we're caught up with family, let's talk business."

"Whoa!" Beau held up a hand. "I came for two reasons, work and Nash. We haven't even talked about him and I think he comes first. What's going on with you two? You broke up?"

"Yes, it's been a few weeks and I may now regret it."

"Tell him. He's a mess without you."

"You think?"

"Let's table the business talk and meet tomorrow at the gym. How about one more drink, we enjoy the ocean and reminisce about old times or anything that will get your mind off Nash for a while?"

"Deal." Vanessa smiled. Beau supported them both, and she loved him for it.

A half hour passed, and Vanessa felt revived. The setting sun, ocean breeze and the smell of the salt water calmed her and helped her come to a decision. "Beau, I was serious earlier about the breakup. I should have thought it through. We're miserable without each other."

"Then, I think we should leave. This is good news. You need to find Nash and tell him. He should be back from his trip by now. Here I thought you'd be crying on my shoulder or asking me why he's always such an ass."

Vanessa laughed and rose from her chair. "You know him well."

Beau walked Vanessa to the valet station. Their cars came within minutes and Beau escorted her to the Mustang. Before getting in, Vanessa turned and gave him a hug. "Thanks, Beau."

Without warning, Beau's body was ripped away from hers and a voice yelled, "What the hell do you think you're doing?"

CHAPTER SIX

"Nash! Stop it!" Vanessa watched in horror as he slammed his friend against the building. She ran to them and pounded on his back. "It's Beau, idiot!"

Nash took a step back and wiped his face. "Beau. Damn, I'm sorry. I thought someone was hitting on Vanessa." He pointed at his friend. "You weren't ... were you?"

"Beau." Vanessa rushed to his side. "Are you okay?"

"I'm fine. Nash has thrown a meaner punch than this one. Besides, he mostly missed." Beau smiled. "I think I better go."

"No, I'm the one who should leave." Nash turned to the valet. "Bring my car back."

"Nash," Beau said. "Stay. We'll go inside and have a drink."

"No." Nash hung his head. "I'll see you back at the house, Beau." He hopped into his Ferrari when it arrived and peeled out of the parking lot.

"That wasn't good." Beau shook his head.

"He believed us, right? There's no way he thought we met for a date." Vanessa watched the Ferrari speed down the street.

"His head is in another place, Van. I'm giving him a pass this time. I'll go to his place and talk to him there."

"No," Vanessa said with a shake of the head. "He won't go home. I know where he's headed."

"Okay, I'll go to his house, and you find him." Beau kissed her cheek. "Good luck."

Vanessa slid behind the wheel and headed for Gill's Gym. Whenever Nash needed to blow off steam he'd work out for hours. She glanced at the time and saw it was almost ten p.m. The nightly gym rats would be there until the midnight closing. She'd stay until then and help shut down for the night. Hopefully, they could talk.

The gym gave off a pale orange glow in the darkness and Vanessa saw people running on treadmills in front of the large picture window as she pulled in the parking lot. She went around back to her spot, letting herself in the private doors with her key. Nash would be on the farthest out-of-the-way treadmill in the place.

"Nash." Vanessa slapped her hands on the front of the machine when she found him. "Look at me."

"No." Nash stared straight ahead.

A flashback of being in the same situation came to Vanessa, but she was avoiding him. She hit the stop button almost making Nash fall off the back of the machine.

"Hey! What'd you do that for?" Nash growled.

"To do this." Vanessa slipped into his arms and planted a kiss on his mouth. She felt his body move against her, his hands on her back tightening their grip as he pulled her closer.

Nash drew back and studied her face. "Does that mean we're back together?"

"No … not yet. I needed to get your attention."

"You have it. So, are we back together?"

"Let's get through this week and next. I'll go to the charity event with you, see how things go and I'll make my decision."

"That's nine days away. I can't wait that long." Nash teased.

"You'll survive."

"Will I?" Nash lifted his brows.

"Maybe not, but I may need to kill you myself if you believe Beau and I were doing something behind your back."

"I didn't know it was Beau, I swear," Nash answered. "I saw you in some guy's arms by the Mustang and flipped out. An explosion went off inside me. All I could think was it should've been me holding you." He hung his head. "I'll apologize to him later. He's at the house, right?"

"Yes. He came here to help me with the event and said he wanted to talk to you, too."

"I remember." Nash nodded. "Hang on." He took an unfamiliar phone from his pocket. "I've got to take this."

Vanessa watched his facial expressions, wondering what type of call he'd get this late at night on a phone she didn't recognize.

"I can't leave now. What? Oh, all right. Fine." Nash looked at her with pleading eyes. "Can we continue this conversation when I get back? I have to leave."

"You need to leave now, this very minute, when we're in the middle of something."

"Yes."

"Why?"

"I can't explain."

"Okay, when will you get back?" Vanessa asked, feeling more irritated by the minute.

"I hope tomorrow night."

"Let's have dinner Saturday night. We can talk then."

Nash bit into his bottom lip. "I'm not sure I can. I may be gone this weekend."

Her stomach tightened into a ball. "Was that a woman on the phone? Did you meet someone in Pittsburgh?"

"What? No!"

"Then you've met someone somewhere and purchased a special phone to contact her. You're leaving now and will be gone this weekend. How stupid do you think I am?" Vanessa threw a hand up in the air. "Forget about us, Nash. Go do your thing. You always do!" She stormed away and up the stairs to her office, locking the door behind her.

In less than a few seconds, Nash pounded on the door. "Vanessa! Come on! Let me explain."

Tears rolled down her cheeks as she leaned against the door. "Go away!"

"No, not until you open the door."

"Then you'll be here all night and I think you have somewhere to be!"

* * * *

"Fuck this shit!"

"Well, hello to you, too." Beau rose from the sofa, beer in hand. "Let me get you a cold one."

"Can't." Nash growled.

"Water?"

Nash made a noise in his throat.

"At least sit down for a minute." Beau paused. "You're still not mad at me?"

"No." Nash let out a breath. "Go ahead. Punch me. Then we're even."

"I will not hit you, Nash. Obviously, you're under a lot of stress. Is Smith doing this to you?"

"Damn right he is! Wait till it's your turn, Beau. Don't come crying to me."

"It seems like he knows how to get to you. Chase acted the same way when we saw him." Beau walked to the small fridge at the bar in the corner of the great room and grabbed a bottled water. "Drink this. Tell me what you can."

"Fine." Nash took the bottle, opened it and downed half. "Vanessa wanted us to get back together but I'm sure you knew. Right in the middle of our talk Smith calls, and I can't tell her who it is. Know what he says?"

"Give her a franchise?" Beau winced.

"No! I have to leave for Pittsburgh tonight."

Beau made a face. "That's your mission? You go to Pittsburgh?"

"Long story. You remember the three guys I interviewed for the franchise?"

"Yeah, there were two black men, and you gave one of them the gym in Charlotte, the army vet. The third was from Cuba. You thought he didn't want to leave Miami and took him off the list."

"Well, I'm helping the ones who didn't get the job. I've probably said too much and Smith will call to tell me to shut up, but that's my assignment."

"I like it. I'm surprised you're not into it. This is something you love to do. What's the problem?"

"Vanessa thought Smith was my new girlfriend calling, someone I met in Pittsburgh. I had to blow her off for the weekend, too, so she's suspicious."

"And, you can't tell her the truth."

"I'm going to talk to Smith about it." Nash ran his hand through his hair. "I've got to get ready to leave. I came home to pack an overnight and let you punch me."

"Tempting as it is?" Beau lifted a shoulder. "Another time. You seem to be in enough pain as it is."

"Hug it out?" Nash lifted a brow and smirked.

"Nah, I'm good." Beau returned to his seat.

"Did you know Kade was in New York City?"

"He'd sent me a message, and I thought I'd talk to him in person this weekend. He's not using my place to crash."

"Maybe he's living at the rental space. Once he gets going on a project someone has to force him to eat. Scrawny kid. He never listens to my food or workout advice."

Beau chuckled. "Most of us don't."

Nash glared at him.

"I'm kidding! In fact, I have plans to stop by Gill's tomorrow to help Vanessa and will probably workout. Is that okay?"

"Yes ... of course!"

"Calm down, big guy. Just checking." Beau glanced at his phone. "Smith's meeting is Saturday at seven pm. Did you get a message?"

"He may have told me when we spoke. I got a text, but I didn't read it yet."

"Hey, don't let your anger cloud your judgment. Did you forget why we're doing this? Change the world for the better, one person at a time. Remember, Mission Impossible. We're all in, Nash."

"You're right as usual, Beau, old buddy. Thanks for reminding me."

"Can I also remind you about a sense of humor you used to have? You'd be humming the movie's theme song by now."

Nash lifted the corner of his mouth. "Not in a joking mood, Beau."

"I hear you. Things will get better, especially once you're done with the mission. You can focus on Van and your relationship. Do you think you'll be back in time from your Pittsburgh meeting to fly to Charlotte with me?"

"I should be. I need to be at a bank somewhere in Pittsburgh first thing tomorrow morning to sign papers. I'll fly back after I'm done."

"Simple as that?"

"It better be or Smith will have to answer to me."

* * * *

The flight to Pittsburgh landed at midnight and Nash grumbled all the way to the hotel. "Smith is doing this on purpose. He's keeping us apart. But if he is, why does he care about Vanessa and me?"

Nash unlocked the door, ordered room service and turned on the TV. Flipping channels, he came to rest on a sports station. To his surprise, C.J. stood with a reporter. "When did that happen?" He scratched at his stubble, pulled off his clothes and jumped on the bed in his boxers. "Vanessa had something to do with this." His phone was in his jeans pocket, and he rolled to the side of the bed searching the pants. "Please pick up," he said after he dialed.

"What?"

"Hello to you, too," Nash said, glad Vanessa couldn't see the smile on his face. *She answered!*

"Sorry. I meant, what do you want?"

"Oh, that's much better," Nash teased. "I'm watching the sports channel."

"What else is new." Vanessa paused. "You saw the interview."

"It's on right now. When did the magic happen?"

"I've got a connection with one of our local sports station guys and offered him an exclusive. The sports channel must have picked it up because it's newsworthy. I hoped that would happen."

"You work fast."

"So do you. Is your girlfriend lying next to you? Let me talk to her and tell her what an ass you can be."

"I'm alone, Van." Nash let out a breath. "If you hadn't locked yourself in the office, I'd have explained. I needed to come to Pittsburgh to sign some papers. I'm helping Derreck Mills with a project. I'm flying right back tomorrow … to you."

"Really?" Her voice softened.

"Yes, I should arrive some time in the afternoon. I'm yours for the rest of the day. We'll do whatever you want, eat at your favorite restaurant, swim, go out on the boat …"

"Your yacht wouldn't like being called a boat," Vanessa said with a laugh. "A sunset cruise might be nice."

"You've got it. I'll call it in."

"We go as friends."

"What?"

"You agreed. We wait until after the charity event. Besides, you still didn't tell me where you have to go on Saturday night. Another girlfriend?"

"Um." Nash bit into his bottom lip. "Chase's."

"Again? Okay, for some stupid reason, I believe you."

"You've made my day, or I should say night. Van, I love you."

"Mm-hmm."

"That's all you got?" Nash grimaced. "No, never mind. We'll do it your way."

* * * *

With the legalities at the bank done, Nash and Derreck went to breakfast.

"Nash, I don't know what to say. You put the land in my name."

"It's your project, Derreck. I trust you."

"Maybe you won't after you hear my new idea."

Nash sat back and widened his eyes. "What?"

"I want to build a community center, not just a gym. A place where people of all ages can come. I'd like to add on a senior center, daycare and a small library at a later date. Imagine the seniors playing with the little ones, reading books and being available to kids who need an ear after school. Some may even help with homework."

"It sounds great, Derreck, but now you need a staff."

"Is it possible to build in stages? First the computer room and gym then slowly add on as we grow?"

Nash thought for a moment. "I have architects who could help you with ideas. I'll send them your way."

"Really? You don't think I'm taking on too much?"

"Did you ever hear the saying, 'If you can dream it, you can build it'?"

"Yeah." Derreck nodded. "I thought I was dreaming too big."

"Never. I wanted my own gym since I was a thirteen-year-old kid. But, there is one major hurdle you need to work on. How will you continue to fund the place and keep it running after the initial donation from me? I'm willing to set up a trust fund for the big things, but what about day-to-day operations?"

"Let me think on it, Nash. You've done more than your share to make this dream real. You've inspired me to think outside the box and reach higher than even I expected. Your charity event has me thinking. I could do the same thing here."

I inspired him? Nash felt a sense of pride. "You'll do great things, Derreck Mills, I'm sure." He reached for the check. "My turn. And, if you don't mind, I have a plane to catch."

Nash's heart pounded on the way to the airport. He felt like a teen with his first crush. Vanessa's face flashed before him as he parked the rental, and he jogged to the private airline waiting room. Surprised to find Andy waiting for him since someone else flew him to Pittsburgh the night before, he slapped him on the back. "Working overtime?"

"Maybe?" Andy pretended to think. "Nah, I love my job. Once I get you home and fly back to Charlotte, I'm meeting my family for a late lunch. So, I don't work all the time. But afterwards, it's back to C.Y."

"Take a long lunch. You deserve it."

The two men walked to the jet and boarded. "You seem in a better mood than the last time I saw you, Nash. Things must have gone well for you this time."

"They did, Andy. Thanks for noticing. Now do me a favor and get me home."

* * * *

"After the hectic week we've had, this is heaven," Vanessa said as Nash's yacht pulled away from his private dock.

A waiter set a bowl of chilled shrimp over ice, a summer salad and glasses of white wine on a table and disappeared.

"Shall we?" Nash offered Vanessa his hand. He had a hard time keeping his eyes off her body.

Clad in a hot pink string-bikini, Vanessa slipped her soft hand in his. She grabbed a sheer black short sleeve blouse and tossed it on, leaving the front open. The wind caught her hair, whipping it in every direction. She took a band from her wrist to wrap it around her dark locks.

They settled in at the table and lifted their glasses. "To us," Nash said. "For a job well done."

"We're not at the finish line yet, big guy. Things are going remarkably well though. I'm glad you made it back in time to go over Robbie's 'demand' list. They've made sure he's never alone, didn't they?"

"Yeah, so?" Nash lifted a brow. "He's a fighter. They always have entourages."

"How are you going to get to him then?"

"What do you mean, Van?"

"I'm not stupid, Nash. You're going to help Robbie and his mom defect."

"Who said so?"

"Me … and Rosa. We figured it out. If we can, they will, too. By the looks of the demands, they already have."

Nash leaned forward, resting his elbows on the table. "I want you to stay out of it, Vanessa. Promise me you will."

"I'm part of Gill's and running the charity event. It would be hard for me to stay out of it, Nash."

"Okay." Nash looked out over the calm waters. "If something goes down, promise you'll run in the other direction."

"As long as no one gets hurt, I will be far, far away from the action." Vanessa winked. "Robbie's camp is coming in on Wednesday. They expect top of the line the whole way." She shook her head. "Are you sure you want to give in to all their demands? Penthouse accommodations for Robbie, Angela and his manager/trainer with separate rooms for the rest."

"Whatever." Nash waved his hand.

Vanessa plucked the last shrimp from the bowl. "Let's lay on the chaise and watch the sun set, Nash."

"On the double?"

"Sure, side by side, but no touching." Vanessa teased.

Their arms made contact, and Vanessa didn't move away. Nash had filled their wineglasses, so they were ready to watch the sun sink to the horizon. The best way to see it go down was from the ocean. Being on the east coast had its perks and sun rises, but the west coast got the evening show.

Vanessa's fingers wove into his as the horizon transformed to pink cotton candy. The golden sun cast a glow as it set, and Nash's heart felt full. *I will fix this, Van, you wait and see.*

CHAPTER SEVEN

"I'll fly back tomorrow morning, promise." Nash lightly brushed Vanessa's lips with his.

"Tell Momma I said hello, Chase, too." Vanessa slipped her arms around his waist. "I loved last night, sleeping on the yacht and driving to the gym together."

"Good. There's more to come."

"And you may get more than a goodnight kiss after next week." Vanessa nudged his chest.

"I like the sound of that." Nash glanced around the gym. "You good here?"

"I'll stay till closing and give Missy and Nathan the night off."

"Make sure someone's in the gym. I don't want you here alone."

"I won't be. I have Pepita." Vanessa joked.

"A damn three-ounce bird locked in its cage will not protect you." Nash kissed the tip of her nose. "I'm talking about a human."

"Victor's usually here."

"I'll make sure."

"No, you go. You have a plane to catch, and I'm sure Beau's already at the airport. I'll talk to Victor."

Nash drank her in one more time before heading to the Ferrari. The meeting started at seven and he knew Chase would have dinner waiting for them. "Make that Renata will have dinner waiting." He chuckled as he slid behind the wheel.

Beau was on the jet when Nash stepped into the cabin. "You made it," he said, looking up from his phone.

"Yep," Nash answered, sitting across from his friend. "Went to Pittsburgh, came home and spent the rest of the time with Vanessa."

"You're back together?" Beau lifted his brow.

"Not yet, but we're close. Vanessa's agreed to be my date to the charity event. She'll decide after it's over." Nash glanced toward the cockpit. "Who's the pilot?"

"Andy's dad." Beau shook his head. "I can't think of his name."

"Andy Senior?" Nash chuckled. "I have no idea either. We're terrible, Beau."

"No, you're terrible, I just can't remember." Beau smiled. 'I'm happy for you, big guy. Your mission is halfway done, and you'll have your girl back by the end."

"You and Van are the only ones I let get away with calling me big guy." Nash narrowed his eyes. "Anyone else?" He made a fist, and Beau laughed.

The plane took off, and they switched to Mission Impossible business.

"Who do you think is next?" Beau asked.

"Last time, I got the feeling it would be me. Kade, maybe?" Nash shook his head. "He's right in the middle of helping a new designer. I can't see Smith pulling him away from that." He pursed his lips. "Yes, I can. He acted like I had time to organize the charity fight, but not really. So why not put Kade in an impossible situation?"

"You don't appear to like Smith anymore," Beau said. "Didn't you want to call the guy Charlie as a joke?"

"You're right. I'm not fond of the man, Beau. He's not a huge help. We also know nothing about him. I keep telling myself he has altruistic motives."

"Said the man from Harvard." Beau pursed his lips.

"You found him, Beau. You never said how you did it." Nash stared at him.

"I wish I knew. We were so drunk I can barely remember."

An announcement came over the speaker. "Mr. Gill? Mr. Miller? Prepare to land."

"Quick! What's Andy's last name?" Nash asked. "We can use it like he did!"

"I can't recall it at this moment!" Beau said in a loud whisper. "Just call him Captain."

Nash thought back to his college days, when he and Beau planned ways get out of an awkward situation. He could always be himself with Beau and never felt judged. Beau sometimes acted as if the weight of the world was on his shoulders, feeling responsible to prove himself in the business world and also take care of his family. He confided in Nash and Nash did the same. Nash would always be there for him and was a better person for knowing Beau. He'd watched Beau transform over the years from serious guy to not being so uptight and hoped he'd played a small part.

The flight attendant opened the door to the plane after they landed and nodded it was okay to leave. Andy's dad stepped from the cockpit extending his hand as Nash and Beau walked toward him.

"Smooth flight, sir," Nash said, shaking his hand and quickly moved on to the attendant.

"Thank you, Captain." Beau followed behind him and Nash felt a nudge to his back.

Nash turned to Beau when they reached the tarmac and gave him a knowing look. "We did it. Good plan. No small talk. It might get us in trouble. Don't stop, keep moving."

They high-fived and walked to the terminal where they found a limo waiting to take them to Chase's. In less than a half hour, the car pulled down the long drive to the house. The woman who'd picked them up, hopped out, opened the back door and wished them a good night.

Nash stopped and inhaled. "Carolina air."

Dogs began to bark and the garage door opened. Renata ducked under the ascending door followed by Chase's two golden retrievers.

"Belle and Bear." Nash crouched down to greet them, scratching them behind the ears.

"You greet the dogs first?" Renata folded her arms yet had a smile on her face. "How is my stubborn daughter?"

"She's fine and sends her love." Nash hugged Vanessa's mom.

The dogs ran down the driveway to greet Beau who'd stayed behind to talk to the driver. *He's probably giving her an extra tip.* Nash shook his head. "Get him, Belle! That a girl."

"Beau!" Renata waved. "Come in the house. Dinner is almost ready."

Nash watched as Beau handed the driver some bills. Belle sat patiently next to him, waiting to escort him up the drive. The dogs were well-trained, happy to see a person but never jumped on them. After the initial greeting, they'd drop to position. Beau bent down and scratched Belle behind the ears. "Come on, girl." They walked up the drive together. "Renata, didn't I just see you?" Beau teased after a hug.

"Yes, but I love when you boys are here. Bear! Get out of the bush. I swear he has to mark his territory everywhere."

"Are the others here yet?" Nash asked as they walked through the garage and up the stairs to the kitchen.

"Gabe and Finn are with Chase. Kade isn't here yet. They're outside on the patio."

"I smell something delicious. Do you need any help?" Nash asked.

"Go." Renata laughed and nudged him and Beau toward the sunroom. "I won't get anything done with you in my kitchen."

When they reached the patio, Beau grabbed two beers from the outdoor fridge nestled into the rocky landscape and handed one to Nash. "Look at Chase," he said under his breath. "What in the hell happened?"

Nash glanced Chase's way and saw he had a bandage above one eye at the hairline. "Damn! I don't know."

"It's about time you got here," Finn said. "Is Kade with you?"

"No, you entitled piece of shit." Nash grinned. He liked to push Finn's buttons.

Finn, the only privileged one in the Society, had roomed with Chase in college. He came from a family of long-time real estate investors. They owned hotels, vacation rentals and built upscale housing divisions. Their list of holdings was long and solid. Finn may have been rich, but he wanted to find his own way. When the six of them discussed the Secret Billionaire Society as a joke, Finn was first onboard.

"This piece of shit is doing well, as always. Thank you for asking," Finn answered. "Have you added more muscle since I last saw you?" He reached for Nash's head.

"Cut it out."

"Hey? Where's your sense of humor, Nash? I was waiting for you to say you'd use the new muscle on me, and I'd take a head butt to the gut or something."

"I'm not in a joking mood."

"He's got a lot on his mind," Beau said, coming to Nash's rescue. "The rest of us will have to wait and see what it's like when we get our assignments."

"Piece of cake." Finn snapped his fingers. "I'll be done in less than two weeks, which seems to be the amount of time we get."

"Barely enough." Nash snarled. He studied his friend.

Finn was of Scandinavian descent, tall and lean, blonde, blue eyes. His family immigrated to America from Sweden over a century ago, ending up in Chicago. His great-grandfather saved every penny and bought or built real estate around town. Finn's grandfather inherited the Larsson Real Estate Corporation and expanded his holdings throughout the country. He opened another office in Los Angeles and set up his son as CEO. Finn was a born and bred California boy.

"Well, look who finally showed up," Finn said when Kade appeared on the patio.

"Hello to you, too, Finn." Kade gave him the finger. They slapped each other on the back as Kade passed by and he continued around the room to greet everyone.

"Chase waited until you got here to tell us about his scar," Gabe said. "Grab a beer and sit."

Nash noticed Gabe opened up once Kade arrived. The two had come from Colorado together to Harvard, rooming in a dorm then moving to an apartment sophomore year. They'd been friends since middle school and the only two who had a longer history than the rest of the group.

Kade squinted at Chase. "What the hell happened?"

"I was in a car accident." Silence filled the patio. "Someone tampered with my brakes, cut the line just enough so the fluid would slowly drip out and for me to make it to the highway."

"You're lucky, man. Just a cut on head?" Kade touched his own forehead.

"A concussion, too, but I've been cleared by a doctor."

"Who did it?" Nash asked. "You know, don't you?"

"Craig." Chase hung his head.

"*Your* Craig?" Finn looked shocked. "Craig Hawk, the guy you hired to run C.Y.?"

"Yes."

"You trusted him," Finn said. "The bastard. I hope he goes to jail for twenty years." He looked around the room. "None of us are lawyers but we're familiar with the laws. What do you get for attempted murder these days?"

"There's more to it," Chase interrupted.

"Than murder?" Finn's face reddened with anger. "Hawk almost killed you."

"I didn't realize it at the time, but Craig was part of my mission. I was supposed to find out about his underhanded dealings with Falcon Airlines on my own. He was buying up shares after he sabotaged the company to make them look bad."

"And for the stocks to drop," Beau added, shaking his head.

"Yeah." Chase acknowledged. "But I saved the day and met someone."

"Holy Jesus, Mary and Joseph!" Finn slapped his cheek. "Has the playboy found someone to tame him?"

Chase gave Finn a hard stare. "I love her and plan to marry her one day."

"When do we meet her, Chase?" Gabe asked.

"In six weeks … I hope. If she'll still have me." Chase grimaced. "Smith's rule."

"F that!" Finn said. He and Gabe preferred not to use bad language to their friends' amusement, but Finn always found a way to make a point with an almost swear.

"See?" Nash pointed at Chase, looking at his other friends. "What did I tell you about Smith?" He glanced back at Chase. "Congrats, by the way, bro. She's a keeper."

"You met her?" Beau's eyes widened.

"Yeah, accidentally …" Nash turned to Chase. "Is she okay with the six-week break?"

"I don't know."

"Dinner's ready!" Renata walked in, carrying a tray, followed by three more servers. "I'll put everything on the table and you can help yourselves. We've got steak, chicken or shrimp kabobs, rice and beans, also some fried yucca."

"Thanks, Renata," Chase said. "It looks and smells delicious, as always."

"Please come to work for me, Renata," Finn begged. "I'll double your salary."

"You know I am perfectly fine working here, Finn." Renata winked. "But, thank you, as always, for the offer."

"Smith arrives at seven?" Kade asked as they gathered round the table.

"That was the message I got," Chase answered. "To tell you the truth, guys, I'm glad I'm done and made it through. I didn't want to let you down. If I'd screwed up the first mission, this would be over."

"And we'd be paupers." Finn laughed.

"We'd have to start over," Nash added. "But I trusted Chase ... and now the rest of you. And, don't worry about me. I'll finish my mission."

"I had no doubts," Kade said. "How's the charity event coming?"

"We're locked in and focused on every detail. Vanessa's done a lot of work in a short period of time. I don't know what I would have done without her."

"She has no clue you're on a mission?" Kade looked at him out of the corner of his eye.

"No, Kade, but it's hard. I can't tell any of you much, either. All I can ask is for you to be in Miami next Saturday to support me even if it's just the six of us at the event."

"I think you'll get more guests than us," Beau said. "This event is picking up steam. I've been watching Twitter and C.J.'s team is doing a fine job of getting the word out. Hashtag Mack Attack, if anyone's interested."

Everyone's phone buzzed, pinged or rang at the same time. They looked at each other, nodded and rose from their chairs. Six guys walked along the stone pathway leading to the bunker to await Mr. Smith.

* * * *

"Well, now we know," Nash said as the five Society members emerged from the interrogation room. "Finn's next. He said he'd beat the two-week record. Good luck trying."

"What really happens in there after we leave?" Gabe asked, gesturing over his shoulder with a thumb.

"Truthfully?" Nash lifted his eyebrows. "Not much. Smith gave me more specifics—names, addresses and the burner phone. Since I knew the guys I'm helping, there wasn't much to talk about."

"Nash!" Chase nudged him in the chest. "Don't tell us details. No one should get the specifics of your assignment."

"Mission Impossible stuff, right?" Nash smiled. "Are you glad yours is over, Chase?"

"Yes, and no. I miss Grace, and I didn't mind flying for Falcon. My co-pilot was great. I'm going to try to steal her away from them and give her Craig's job."

"Son of a bitch," Nash said. "I can't believe he did that to you. Why didn't you call us? The five of us would've given him a beat down to remember."

"That's exactly why." Chase chuckled. "A toast is needed to celebrate my completed mission. Shots for everyone."

"Make mine a double." Finn said, slamming the interrogation room door behind him. All eyes went to him, waiting for more. "I don't care what Smith says, this assignment is B.S."

"Did he say something like 'dig deeper'?" Chase asked.

"Or there is always more to an assignment than 'that's it'?" Nash added.

"What? No." Finn wrinkled his brow. "I'm to fly back to LA tomorrow. He'll send directions to my phone. I'm supposed to get in my car and follow the GPS. I wasn't given any more details."

"It's the least information given yet." Chase rubbed above his eye.

"Are you okay, Chase?" Beau asked. "You said you're recovering from a concussion. At least sit down."

"Thanks, Beau. I think I will." Chase glanced at Finn. "Join us. You can have as many shots as you want, but you'll be on a plane to LA tomorrow if we have to drag you."

The mood lightened as the night wore on. Sensitive to their friend's recent concussion, the guys kept the music low and another *Mission Impossible* movie on silent. Chase fielded as many questions as possible until he held up his hands and said, "Enough!"

Kade hopped from his seat, holding one arm in the air, helping to change the mood. "Six!" he shouted.

Finn, Nash, Gabe and Beau followed his lead. Chase joined the circle, completing the pyramid they fashioned with their arms, their secret signal, and they chanted, "From the bottom to the top!"

In college, Beau had created a special pyramid to represent the Society and also an emoji for them to use. Sometimes they'd send the pyramid to each other and nothing else … just because.

"Remember," Chase said. "The pyramid is ours and ours alone. Only we recognize what it stands for or what it means to us."

By midnight, pizzas were delivered, and everyone dove into the boxes.

"Feeding the wolf pack was a good idea, Chase," Kade said as he took one more slice. "If I can speak for the rest of us," he said as he gestured to Beau and Gabe, "we're just as on edge as you guys on assignment."

"Only worse," Gabe said. "We don't know our missions."

Nash felt his phone vibrate and rose to answer in a quieter place. His screen flashed, "Vanessa".

"Van? Everything all right?"

"Yes, I figured you'd still be awake. I wanted to tell you everything went smoothly here. The gym rats have left for the night, I let Victor out the door and remembered I forgot to change Pepita's water."

"So, you called me cause you're alone in the gym now."

"Yeah, don't be mad, I knew you wouldn't like it. It's less than an hour of alone time, the cleaning crew comes in at one."

"You're not planning to stay, are you?" Nash tried to keep his voice low so the others wouldn't hear.

"No, I'm already in my office. Pepita say hello to daddy."

Nash hated when she said he was Pepita's father and knew she did it on purpose. "I'm not a damn bird, Van."

"Aww, did you hear her? She chirped hello. One more minute."

He heard water running and the snap of the cage door. "You done?"

"Yes, I'm on the stairs."

"You got the nighttime lighting on yet?"

"Yes, I thought I was leaving. What's the big deal anyway? I come to the gym at five every morning. and you don't seem to mind."

How can I tell her what I don't know myself? I'm worried but have no idea why. Nash had a feeling Vanessa would get caught up in his assignment, and now she was squarely in the middle. He was guilty of letting her in with no details. At least he could protect her. *From what? Just a feeling, but a bad one.*

"Nash? You still there?" Vanessa whispered.
"Yes, what's wrong?"
"I heard a noise. It's probably nothing."
Nash's heart raced. "Call nine-one-one, Van."
"I said it was nothing …"
"Van?"
"I heard it again," she whispered, then yelled, "Who's there?"

"Don't call out and give them your location," Nash hissed. "Van? Did you hear me? Are you there?"

CHAPTER EIGHT

Nash raced into the room. "Chase, get me on a plane. Now!" He fumbled with his phone, trying to locate the number for the Miami Beach police in his contact list.

Chase walked straight to the house phone, and Beau jumped from the sofa. "I'm going with you, Nash. Don't argue."

"Fine. Get us a car."

"Take the Audi," Chase said from the other side of the room.

"I'll go get it." Beau jogged to the door and Nash frantically paced around the room.

Gabe took him by the arm and guided him to where Chase stood. "Wait here. See what he says then I'll walk you to the garage."

Nash wanted to say he wasn't a baby, but the look on Gabe's face was so sincere, he said, "Thanks." He held up his pointer finger when he heard a voice on the phone. "Bruce? Yeah, Nash Gill. Vanessa's over at the gym by herself, and I'm not in town. Could you send a car over?" He paused. "Thanks."

Chase hung up and looked at Nash. "Go. Plane will be fueled and ready when you get there. Good luck." He shook Nash's hand. "I'll see you next Saturday in Miami."

Gabe held the door open and waved to Nash. "Come on."

Nash would never admit he was glad Gabe had offered to come but was glad someone walked with him. "Gabe, you're a great guy. Can I ask you something?" he asked on their way to the garage.

"Sure, if it helps distract you."

"You've always been the quiet one of the group especially if Kade hasn't shown up yet. Are you okay hanging with us?"

"You want to talk about me, Nash?" Gabe chuckled. "I should be the last thing on your mind."

"You said I needed a distraction." Nash elbowed him in the side. I noticed tonight you didn't have much to say until Kade arrived."

"I've known Kade a long time. Maybe I'm more comfortable when he's around." Gabe shrugged. "It's just that …"

"Come on!" Beau called from the driver's side window. "Hop in."

"You gonna be all right?" Gabe stared at Nash, looking concerned.

"Not until I land in Miami."

"Take care, brother." Gabe slapped him on the shoulder and turned to Beau. "Drive safely."

As soon as Nash slid into the passenger seat, Beau took off down the drive. "Don't get a speeding ticket, dude," Nash told him.

"I don't plan to. I'll get alerts on my phone if any cops are nearby." Beau was out on the street, heading to the highway at an elevated speed. "What's up with Gabe?"

"I thought the same thing. There's something wrong."

"I always thought he was a quiet guy, but there's more to it."

"Yeah," Nash agreed. "Not the best time to confront him while we're in the middle of Mission Impossible."

"I have a theory."

"Of course you do." Nash chuckled although his nerves felt like they burned through his skin.

"We met Kade and Gabe sophomore year when we moved into the same apartment complex. Kade was easy going, and we got to know him first. Maybe Gabe thinks Kade brought him along. *We* didn't recruit him."

"That's bullshit, Beau, and Gabe should know it. He qualified to be in the Society, besides being a great guy."

"Just a theory, big guy."

Nash let out a breath. "You could be right. You're good at reading people, Beau. When this is over, let's invite him to Miami. Hang out."

"The three of us?" Beau gave Nash a quick glance.

"Yeah, we can talk about it when he comes for the charity event."

"We're here." Beau guided the car as close to the airport waiting room as possible.

Nash put his hand on his friend's arm. "I appreciate all you've done but you're not coming with me. Go back to Chase's, get a good night's sleep and head back to New York as you planned. I'll keep you in the loop."

Beau went for his door handle. "You're not getting rid of me this easily."

"Beau, come on. I've got this. My car's in the lot at the Miami airport. I'll be fine."

"All right." Beau sank back into the driver's seat. "Text me, call me, whatever the time." He gave Nash a soulful look. "I hope Van's okay."

* * * *

"Hello? Who's there?" Van dropped her phone into her gym bag and searched for her pepper spray. She headed for the rear of the gym. "Victor?" *I locked the door. He couldn't have come back in.*

Vanessa got to the boxing hall and paused. The staff exit to the parking lot was at the end of it. She peeked around the corner, saw no one and slid along the wall toward the opening of the room as the hair on her arms stood at attention. "If you don't answer or come out now, I'm warning you, I have a weapon. I also put a call into the police. They should be here any minute." *I'm lying about the police, but you can't be sure if I did or not.*

An average height, slim teen stepped from the boxing room, hands in the air. "I ain't got no weapons, lady."

"Turn around." Vanessa approached and patted his sides and checked the waist of his jeans. "Who are you? I've never seen you around here before."

"I'm doing Ricky a favor."

"Ricky?"

"Enrique Dorado, Victor's nephew. I'm a friend of his. He couldn't pick up his uncle tonight, so I offered. He told me to go to the boxing room, and that's where I'd find Victor."

Vanessa wasn't quite sure she believed his story. "How'd you get in?"

"Front door. People were coming out to the parking lot, the lights dimmed, and I thought I better get inside."

"And?"

"I went straight to the boxing room like I was told but Victor wasn't there. I sat down to wait for him."

"What did you say your name was?" Vanessa's heart pounded. She didn't trust the kid and knew she locked the door behind the last couple to leave the building.

"You know what? Maybe Ricky did come, and I've wasted my time and yours. I'll be going." He jutted his thumb toward the staff exit.

"I have to let you out." Vanessa took a mental picture of the teen, pencil mustache, a space between his two front teeth, square-shaped face, shifty brown eyes, slicked-back dark hair, olive skin while she kept her distance. "Stand over there." She pointed to a spot well away from her and quickly unlocked the door, aiming the can of spray at him. "There. Go."

"Have a good rest of the night." The teen nodded. "And, again, I'm sorry if I scared you."

Vanessa didn't wait a second, locked the door and rushed to the boxing room. Victor had a small desk in the corner where he kept his laptop and important papers. *No laptop in sight.* After a careful search, she threw her bag on the desk and dug for her phone. When she found it, she punched in Victor's number.

"Hello, Vanessa?"

"Victor, are you still waiting for your ride, and do you have your laptop?"

"Yes, I have the laptop. I always take it with me. Ricky picked me up like he always does. I'm in his car now."

"Ask him if he asked a friend to pick you up at the gym tonight." She waited, tapping her foot.

"No, he would never. Ricky's a responsible boy."

"Did he talk about his cousin Robbie to his friends? Mention the fight?" Again, she had to wait for them to discuss.

"Yes, he is very proud of his cousin."

"The fight, Victor. Did he say anything about it?"

"Give me one more moment, Vanessa." She heard their voices in the background. "He forgot he wasn't to mention it yet. Kids."

"I know." Vanessa let out a breath. "One more question. Does Ricky have a friend with a pencil mustache and a space between his front teeth?"

Vanessa paced the room while she gathered her thoughts, her eyes searching every corner until they came to rest on the security camera. She walked closer, thinking it looked strange. Someone had placed a piece of duct tape over the lens. Her stomach flipped, yet she kept composed. During the wait, she dragged a chair to the spot, climbed and ripped the gray strip from the camera.

"Vanessa?"

"Yes, I'm here."

"He knows who you are talking about, but Cord is no friend. Just an acquaintance."

"Thanks, Victor."

"Is there a problem?"

"No, I noticed your laptop was missing and wanted to check." She hesitated to tell him she caught Cord in the boxing room after hours. Victor might pass the information to Ricky and it would get back to the teen. She had to keep up the act even as her heart pounded and the blood rushed at high speed through her veins. "I'll talk with you the next time you're here."

"Well, that will be as soon as we open tomorrow." Victor chuckled. "C.J. is training nonstop."

"Okay. I'll be here, too." After she hung up, Vanessa walked the perimeter of the room. "What was he looking for?" She ended up at the desk.

Someone had shuffled the papers on top while some lay on the floor. "I don't think Victor is this messy." She sat in his chair to sort out the facts she'd learned, resting her elbow on the desk, head in her hand. A sudden jolt startled her as her elbow slipped from the top. "Oh! I must have dozed off."

The clock on the wall showed one a.m. Noises in the hall told Vanessa the cleaning crew had arrived. Too exhausted to drive home, she thought she'd curl up on the loveseat in her office.

The head of the crew poked his head in the door. "Oh! Sorry, Vanessa, I didn't know you were still here."

"I'm staying, Frank. Leave my office untouched, please."

"You got it, and I'll make sure the weekend staff is aware you're up there when they come in."

"Thanks." Vanessa ran her hand through her hair. "Good night."

* * * *

Nash busted through the back door of the gym, rushed down the hall and came to a screeching halt in the main room. The cleaning crew was busy at work wiping down the equipment, polishing the floors and vacuuming like normal. "What the …" He glanced around, finding the head of the crew talking to one of his employees. "Frank?"

Frank looked away from the woman and nodded. "I'll be right there, Nash."

The rage he felt during the trip and drive to the gym still consumed him. If Frank didn't have answers, he might explode. *This is not Frank's fault. Don't take it out on him.* He willed the man to hurry.

"Sorry, new employee. What can I do for you?"

"Vanessa."

"She's upstairs sleeping."

"What?" Nash lifted his brows. "Did the police show up?"

"Not that I know?" Frank shrugged.

Nash dialed his contact at the station. "Bruce? Yeah, what happened? Did you send a car?"

"We did. Nothing looked suspicious, and the place was locked. No one answered the door. My guy sat in the car for fifteen minutes then deemed it safe."

"He saw nothing?"

"No."

"Thanks, Bruce." Nash ended the call and turned to Frank. "You said Vanessa is sleeping in her office?"

"She was here when we arrived and looked tired. I'm glad she decided to stay. I told her we'd be here and not to worry."

Nash glanced at his watch. *Two-thirty in the morning. I don't care how tired she is, I'm waking her up.* He bounded up the stairs and knocked on her door. "Vanessa?" He didn't have much patience left but relief had taken the place of rage. "Peaches?" He hoped she'd swing back the door and say not to call her that name. "I'm coming in."

Turning the handle and pushing the door back, Nash found her curled up on her sofa. He pulled a chair up to the edge of the couch and sat looking at her sleeping form and didn't have the heart to wake her. His head bobbed a few times as he sat in the quiet room, and he had trouble keeping his eyes open, but no one could convince him to leave. He'd stay and watch her sleep, guarding her from whoever dared break into Gill's Gym.

* * * *

When Vanessa awoke the next morning, she found Nash sound asleep in a chair in front of her, head flopped to one side and a little drool in the corner of his mouth. "Oh, big guy, you came," she whispered. She sat up, flipped her hair from her eyes and reached over to touch his knee. "Nash?"

"What?" His body jerked as he fell forward, but he caught himself in time. "Van! You're okay. Why didn't you answer your phone? I called every chance I got until I arrived at the gym." Nash rubbed the back of his neck to get the kinks out and rolled his shoulders a few times.

"I fell asleep in the boxing room and turned off my phone when I got up here."

"Never do that again!" Nash ran his hand through his hair. "I want every detail from the point when we lost contact."

When Vanessa finished her story, she could tell Nash was going over the details in his head. "What are you thinking?" she asked.

"This Cord kid showed up out of nowhere. He wanted something."

"I thought the same thing. I didn't recognize him, Nash. Never saw him."

"I should've let Beau come with me. One of his tech divisions is Cyber security and everything in-between."

"Aww, Beau wanted to come?"

"He's my best friend, Van. He thought I didn't have many brain cells left after your call last night and needed someone to do my thinking for me."

"I must thank him."

"Get your stuff. You're staying at my house until the charity event."

Is he trying to move me into his house so I'll never leave? No, Nash isn't like that. He's concerned and being sweet. "I can't, Nash. Besides, Pepita would be jealous."

"You can bring her." Nash pursed his lips. "I hate to say it, but the bird may not even be safe here."

"What?" Vanessa placed her hand on her throat. "Would you still take her if I don't come?"

"Yes." Nash leaned forward and kissed her. "Anything for you."

Her heart melted but her head remained firm. "Her cage won't fit in your Ferrari." She teased.

"Very funny. I'll call home and someone on staff will come and get her."

"You don't have to do this." Vanessa closed one eye and stared at him. The image of Cord flashed before her, and she changed her mind. "But I appreciate it."

"One less thing for you to worry about, Van." Nash moved to the couch and rubbed her back.

"Ooh, that feels good after sleeping on this tiny sofa." His hand traveled up into her hair, massaging her scalp. Vanessa got lost in the feeling but only for a minute. "Great! Thanks." She hopped from the sofa. "I need to talk to Victor."

"After you do, you're going home to rest." Nash reached for her hand. "Take the day off."

"You never do."

"It's time we started." Nash kissed the top of her hand. "Go. Work from home if you must."

"I will come over later to visit Pepita and make sure she's in a good spot." Vanessa touched his cheek. "Thank you for coming to my rescue."

"You didn't need rescuing," Nash smirked.

"I know." Vanessa winked and left the office to hunt down Victor.

"There you are," Victor said when he spotted her. "You had me worried last night."

"Your laptop was missing and since Cord was in the building …"

Victor's eyes widened as he covered his mouth. "Cord was here after hours?"

"Yes, and please don't share anything we say with Ricky. For his safety, I don't want him involved."

"Neither do I. When I mentioned a kid with a pencil mustache his jaw tightened, and his muscles twitched. Not a good sign. Cord may run with the wrong crowd, and Ricky needs to stay on his good side. My brother taught him well, Vanessa. Do not worry."

"Look at your desk." Vanessa gestured toward it. "Is it the way you left it?"

"What?" Victor shook his head as he glanced at the mess. "I haven't been over to check it yet but it looks like a tornado hit the top."

"Cord must have been going through your papers looking for some information."

"I do not understand. Why would a kid from Miami care about what is going on in the gym?"

"Perhaps Cord's into gambling and wants details for the fight. Or … he could be working for the other side."

CHAPTER NINE

Nash waited until he saw Vanessa leave the gym, locked his office door and dialed Smith.

"Good morning, Mr. Gill."

"It hasn't been a good morning for me, Smith."

"It appears you have arrived back to Miami safely, so I would assume it is. Is everything all right?"

"No, everything is not all right! You know damn well it isn't. This mission is dangerous. We didn't ask to get killed *or* for you to put our loved ones in harm's way."

"Of course not. I have to admit this mission is riskier, but the rewards are greater."

"Is that your 'Confucius says' quote for the day?"

"Confucius was a great Chinese philosopher who emphasized moral correctness."

"I don't need a history lesson now. Tell me, how do I pull this off with no one getting hurt?"

"Confucius say, 'Never give a sword to a man who can't dance.'"

"What the hell does that mean?" Nash planned to go downstairs and pound a punching bag after the conversation ended. "Smith? Did you hear me? Are you giving me a clue? Are you even there? Damn!" He hung up, threw his cell on his desk and stared into space. "Never give a sword to a man who can't dance. You know what, Smith? All my friends can dance."

An idea hit him as he deciphered the clue. Nash rushed around to the other side of his desk. He grabbed a tablet and pen, writing each Society member's name and their strengths. One thing he was sure, they held their own in a fight. Each had a concealed weapon permit from states Florida would accept. They kept their skills sharp and knew how to use a gun. He needed them to carry at the party. "I have a security team for functions, but these guys … I trust." He stared at the paper, deciding it couldn't wait. He had to tackle the issue now. He grabbed his phone and sent them the emoji of the pyramid. "Let them wonder why I sent it, but they'll know I need them."

Finn might already be on a plane to California but after checking the time, Nash saw it was still early. Everyone had to be at Chase's, and after last night's partying, he assumed they still were. *Where would they go? They all have rooms there. They'll be together. An added bonus.* He put in a call to Chase despite the early hour.

"What the hell time is it?" Chase groaned.

"Good morning to you, too, sweetheart." Nash chuckled. "I need your help."

"At seven a.m. on Sunday?" Chase groaned. "Wait, let me start over. What do you need?" He paused. "I just saw the message. The pyramid. Things that bad?"

"Are the guys still there?"

"Yeah. Finn leaves at nine if I can sober him up enough to get him on a plane."

"Can you get them to the bunker and call me back?"

"Give me a half hour. Sounds like you need our help for your mission."

"You're aware I can't tell you details, but yes, I do need help. Tell them we will put the Pyramid into action. We need all hands-on deck to make this work."

"Will do. Hey, sorry, I forgot to ask. Is Vanessa okay? I said nothing to Renata."

"Yes, she's fine and thanks for not telling her mom. Something suspicious went down here last night. I don't like it, but I haven't figured out why some guy broke into the gym and pretended he was there to give Victor a ride home."

"Victor? He was one of your finalists for the franchise, right? The Cuban guy I flew to Charlotte along with the other two?"

"Yeah, you have a good memory."

"Smith tasked you with helping the remaining two, the ones you didn't choose. That's why you were so mad when you came out of the interrogation room."

"I was being stupid. I thought we'd all get to change our names and go undercover like you."

"Sorry."

"Don't be. One of my missions is turning out to be riskier than I thought."

"And the reason you need us. I'll get back to you soon," Chase said as he hung up.

Nash inhaled deeply, feeling better after talking to Chase. "Time to clean up and start the day."

Vanessa may have her own bath and dressing area at the gym, but Nash had a bedroom and bath. He unlocked the door to his private quarters and headed for the shower, deciding he had time before the guys called. *What will I tell them? Pack heat but don't ask why? I'm glad Chase has figured out some of the mission.*

With only a few hours sleep, the shower helped revive him. He wished he could linger and think of the times he shared this bathroom with Vanessa. The best moments were in hers, smelling of peaches and cream, and washing each other's hair. Sometimes they'd have sex, but not always. Being close to her, feeling her wet skin against his and light conversation were more intimate. Nash knew every inch of her mind and body. *Well, almost.*

Nash dressed in Gill's gym wear, gray polo, shorts and orange sneakers. "Better get out to the office. Call's coming soon." A thought nudged him, but he lost it until he sat at his desk. "Pepita!"

Using the office phone, he quickly dialed the head of his staff. "Carl?" He waited as the man updated him on the day-to-day running and needs of the house. "I want you to send someone, no make that two people, in a van to come to the gym. Their job is to take Pepita to the house. Find a good spot for her. Vanessa will stop by later to check on the bird. Will you stop laughing? Just get someone over here. I've got to go. Thanks, Carl."

Nash shuffled papers on his desk, not really concentrating on business. He wanted answers about this kid, Cord, and knew Beau was his man. Beau may have started out dreaming of owning a tech company, but his instincts were for Cyber security and detective work. The office building he'd owned and renovated in Upper Manhattan had floors for each business venture he'd started.

Beau reserved the top two floors for personal living space. Every Society member had a room on the floor below Beau's penthouse. "Funny thing is, Beau, you rarely live there." Nash chuckled and shook his head. "You like to go home to Brooklyn."

His cell rang, and Nash put it on speaker. "Chase?"

"Yeah, we're all here. Hung over, but here."

"Beau? I'd like to talk to you later when we finish."

"You got it," he answered. "Speaking for all of us, we're glad Vanessa is safe. We saw the pyramid, too. Chase said there's more to it, so start talking."

Nash tried to describe without giving too much away what had happened to Vanessa. "I took it as a sign. There might be trouble at the charity event. I'm asking all of you to bring your weapons. We'll pick a designated meeting place before the party starts, and if I need you before the fight, you'll get a pyramid."

"You're supposed to help the boxer, Robbie Dorado, defect, aren't you, Nash?" Gabe asked. "You don't have to say anything. We've been discussing the reasons you're having the charity event."

"We all agree, Nash," Chase added. "Victor's kid is linked to some mob or criminals which makes this dangerous."

Nash was glad they didn't video chat. If his friends saw his face, they'd see a mix of relief and concern. "I'm glad you guys get it." He paused. "Of course, you do. We planned Mission Impossible together. When do you plan to fly in?"

"Most of us should be there Friday," Chase answered. "Finn? I can't say yet."

"If he can't make it, it's okay. I *completely* understand."

"Hey, quit talking about me like I'm not here," Finn piped in. "Give me one week. Piece of cake."

"Finn needs to get to the airport," Chase said. "Any of you have questions before we disconnect?"

Nash heard grumblings in the background, and Finn protesting he could speak for himself. The noises died down, and Beau came on the line. "They're gone, Nash. I told Chase to leave the line open. What's up?"

"I want you to do a background check on someone. Hopefully, you'll have information by this evening."

"What's the name?"

"Cord."

"That's all you got?" Beau's voice climbed a notch.

"I can give you a description, the area where he lives and an acquaintance."

"An acquaintance." Beau sounded frustrated. "Write it up in an email and send it to me. I'll get a team right on it, and before you can say anything … yes, I will personally supervise it."

"Thanks. It's been a long day, Beau."

"It's eight a.m., Nash." Beau laughed. "Go home and get some rest. Let the gym run itself for a change."

"Maybe I will."

* * * *

Vanessa cranked the air, headed for her bedroom and snuggled under a quilt yet Cord kept haunting her mind. *I will never forget that face. A nap is what I need to wipe it from my memory.*

As she slipped into a light sleep, Vanessa's dream took her poolside at Nash's. She sat in a lounge, cold drink in hand, watching him swim laps. He'd dove into the deep end after making love to her, and she smiled knowing he wore no clothes. His head bobbed in and out of the water and she waited in anticipation to see his face again. He swam to the edge of the pool, apparently finished with laps and smiled up at her. The gap between his teeth gave her a start and when Vanessa focused on the rest of his face, she realized it wasn't Nash. *No!* She couldn't believe her eyes! *Cord! What have you done with Nash?*

Vanessa sat up drenched in a cold sweat. "It was a dream. That's all it was. Calm yourself, Vanessa."

Not able to sleep, she slipped from the bed and roamed the apartment. *Maybe Nash is right. I should move in with him until the event. No! I can take care of myself.* She wandered into the kitchen, made a fruit smoothie and sat at the counter. Checking the time, Vanessa decided she had time to hit some of her favorite stores for something new to wear, come home and change before going to Nash's.

Her phone rang as she was heading out the door. "Ro?"

"Yeah, it's me. We flew home yesterday. I thought I'd hear from you. When do you want me to report for work? I can come any time tomorrow."

"Tomorrow?" Vanessa's head swam with details of the night before. She couldn't put her sister in jeopardy.

"It will be Monday, the first day of the week. We only have five days to make this the greatest event of the summer."

"I may have spoken too soon, Rosa. I should've asked Nash before hiring you." *That's it. Blame Nash.*

"*Nash* has a problem, or do you?"

"Can I call you back later today after I see him?"

"You know what, Vanessa? Don't bother. Obviously, I was wrong about earlier this week. I thought we put the feud or whatever it was behind us, but you've had second thoughts. Sorry, I tried to push my way into your precious territory."

"Whoa! You're taking this way too far, Ro."

"No, I'm probably not taking it far enough. I'll be civil at the charity event because Mama will be there, and Kade is making me a fabulous dress. After that? I'll stay in my lane and out of yours. Deal?"

"Fine." When Rosa got this worked up, there was no reasoning with her.

Vanessa didn't feel much like shopping after the phone call but robotically walked to her car and drove to her favorite store. She'd look there, and if she found nothing, she'd come home. An urge to call Nash and tell him about the crazy conversation with Rosa took over, but Vanessa pushed it aside. *I don't need to cry to Nash. I'll see him tonight.*

A few hours later, armed with bags from the store, Vanessa carried all of them at once into the apartment, kicking the door open with her foot after she unlocked it. Dropping packages on the floor, she sat in the middle of the bags, opening boxes of shoes, pulling tags off clothes and jewelry, tossing them everywhere. *Why does shopping make you feel better? Or did I buy all this stuff because I felt bad?*

Tears rolled down her cheeks as she studied the mess. Vanessa dug her hands into her hair and let out a frustrated scream. She pounded the area rug with her fists, wanting everything to go back to normal. Her sister was mad, Nash messed with her mind and Cord scared her. "I'm never afraid of someone like him," she whispered. "Why can't I stop thinking about what happened last night?"

Vanessa gathered up the boxes, stacking them by the chair. She threw the tags and garbage away, grabbed a tight-fitting turquoise dress with scooped-neck from the pile and headed to her bedroom. Traffic should be light since it was Sunday and she'd be at Nash's in ten minutes.

* * * *

Nash double-checked Pepita. He had the bird in his climate-controlled sunroom, not directly in the sun, with fresh food and water. "Alive and well. See, Pepita? I'm able to take care of you with no help."

The bird gave him a cheerful chirp and jumped onto her swing, making him laugh. "If only life could be that simple."

"Now you're having conversations with Pepita. I knew it'd happen." Vanessa joined him, giggling.

Nash had to hold himself back. Vanessa wore a stunning dress which showed her every curve. The color reminded him of the ocean on a sunny, calm day. "You look nice."

"Thanks." Vanessa settled into one of the sunroom's padded chairs. "I love this room. You don't use it enough."

"We can stay here until dinner is ready. Then, we'll head out to the pool."

"Will your parents be coming to the gala?" Vanessa asked.

"Um." Nash had forgotten about them since Mission Impossible started.

"You did invite them?"

Nash was an only child whose parents had indulged him since he remembered. They encouraged him to play football, but when he gave it up, they supported and helped him through Harvard. To repay them, once Nash had made his money, he bought his dad his dream home in Key West and gave him enough cash so he could retire. His parents rarely came up to Miami, loving their new life in the Keys.

"Nash?"

"No, I forgot, but there's still time."

"Call them now."

"I'll do it after you leave … unless you plan to stay." Nash lifted his brows.

"No, I'm going home."

"This could be your home, Van." Nash spread out his arms. "All of this. Redecorate, make it your own, the sky's the limit."

"Don't get ahead of yourself, big guy. We haven't gotten through our fundraiser date. Let's see how that goes first. You agreed."

'Fine. Thirsty?"

"A cold one sounds good." Vanessa let out a breath. "I need to talk to you."

Nash sent a text asking for someone to bring craft beers to the sunroom. "You look upset. Did something more happen?"

"Rosa called me and asked what time she should come to work tomorrow. A strange feeling crept over me and I felt this need to protect her. After what happened at the gym, I'm afraid for her safety."

"Did you tell her?" Nash hoped not. The more people who knew, the worse it could get.

"No, of course not. She'd tell Mama even if I asked her not to say anything. Ro's mad at me now. I told her not to come in and didn't even have time to make up an excuse. You know how Ro is, Nash. She gets angry and there's no talking to her."

"It's probably better this way, Van. Let her stay mad until the event. Afterward, when Robbie and his mom are safe, you can tell her everything. She'll forgive you."

"I thought the same thing." Vanessa exhaled, placing her hand on her stomach. "You and I think alike, Nash. Thanks for the validation."

One of Nash's staff brought beers, chips and salsa into the room and said, "Cook said dinner will be ready in a half hour." He placed the tray on the sunroom table.

"Thanks." Nash nodded and walked to the table. "Want to join me or should I bring it to you?"

"I'll come to the table, although this chair feels mighty comfortable." Vanessa smiled and rose from the seat.

"You look better … happier." Nash ran a finger down her arm when she sat next to him.

"I am. Nothing a long, hot shower couldn't fix. I felt overtired, frustrated, and a little shook up after last night."

"I don't blame you. I put in a call to Beau. He's looking into every Cord in the area. In fact, I should get news while you're here."

"Oh, that'd be awesome."

"I told him to call anytime. I'll put him on speaker." Nash's phone buzzed. "What do you know? It's Beau. He sent me a text and four pictures. It says, 'If Vanessa's with you, ask if she recognizes any of these. I'll begin the investigation once she ID's the guy.'" He brought up the first picture and showed her.

"No." Vanessa shook her head. She didn't recognize number two or three either.

When Nash held up the last one, he watched as her expression changed to a look of fear.

"That's him." Vanessa nodded. "I'd recognize those teeth anywhere."

CHAPTER TEN

"Teeth?" Nash turned the phone to look at the screen. "Oh."

The guy in the photo had a gap between the front two. His smile didn't appear friendly, almost like he'd been forced to make a nice face before they took picture. Nash dashed off another text to Beau and took Vanessa's hand. "You okay?"

"What is it about him, Nash? I can handle any guy in the gym, but this one scares me."

"I have to admit, he scares me a little too." Nash showed her the photo again. "Doesn't this look like a posed picture?"

"A school photo perhaps? Beau must have access to a yearbook or school records."

"Yeah." Nash thought back to his conversations with Victor. "Ricky, Victor's nephew, graduated this year from high school. Cord and Ricky attended school together, so Beau may have started by checking those records."

"Cord doesn't seem like the type who dedicated his life to schoolwork. He's out for himself." Vanessa lifted a shoulder. "Just saying."

Beau's call and the announcement that dinner was ready occurred at the same time. Nash put his friend on speaker as he and Vanessa walked out to the cabana by the pool. The staff had tied the sides to the poles, and a gentle breeze added just enough air to make the evening pleasant. He'd asked for the tiki torches to be lit early, and their flames reflected in the pool. A perfect dinner was being interrupted by business, Mission Impossible business. Nash wasn't too thrilled about that part. Yet, after hearing Vanessa's story and how she feared this guy, he was all in. Adding to the stress, his emotions were all over the place, ones he didn't know he had, and he blamed Smith.

"Nash, now it's my turn to ask, are you okay?" Vanessa's fingers brushed his arm.

"What? Me? Yeah, fine."

"Beau said he'd call back if you wanted."

"No," Nash answered, helping Vanessa to her seat. "Beau, give us a minute."

The kitchen had prepared a cold meal at his request, a pasta alfredo salad with peapods and salmon. A bottle of white wine and crusty bread were in the middle of the table. He served Vanessa and continued around to the other side of the table. "Go ahead, Beau. We're listening."

"Cordero Owens, nineteen, dropped out of high school his junior year. He hangs with a rough crowd and it appears he is their leader. He's got a rap sheet, been to juvie, doesn't seem to care about family. He left home as soon as possible. His father is white. Mother is Puerto Rican. Both factory workers. Cord is the oldest of five and, as I said, moved out when he turned eighteen, either by choice or kicked out."

"Not the best life," Vanessa said.

"No reason to act like a criminal," Nash replied.

"There is abuse in the family," Beau continued. "The police have arrested both father and son for fighting."

"Each other?" Vanessa asked.

"Yeah." Beau paused. "Nash, if you ask me, the kid could be bought. But, the question remains, how did Robbie's people get to him so fast? The other reason he was in the gym? He was searching for clues about the fight. Van might be right. He's into gambling."

"Make sure the guys have his picture, Beau. We'll talk later."

"That was a little unsettling." Vanessa shivered.

"Let's forget about Cord and focus on us." Nash lifted his wineglass. "To us pulling off the feat of the century."

Vanessa stared at him, her lips a thin line.

"What?"

"Exactly …" She closed one eye. "What have you done so far?"

"Paid for everything?"

"Okay, I'll give you that." Vanessa laughed.

"I approved the menu, liquor, hired security and made sure my friends will be there."

"Oh, we couldn't have an event without them." Vanessa rolled her eyes.

Her reaction surprised Nash and he said in a soft voice, "I thought you liked them."

"I do. I'm sorry, Nash. I'm overtired. After dinner, I'll head for home."

"I'll come with and make sure you get in safely." Nash longed for her to stay, even if it was in a separate bedroom like she had on the yacht. He'd feel better knowing her whereabouts.

"If you insist."

"I do." *She didn't fight me. Van is really scared. Maybe I should go find this Cordero and beat the living shit out of him.*

"You have a black evening suit, Nash, but have you ordered a tie?"

"Kade's making me one to match your dress. They will deliver everything on Thursday in case alterations are needed."

"Listen to you." Vanessa teased. "You're talking fashion."

"Come here." Nash patted his knee.

Vanessa slid from her chair, walked to where he sat and let him pull her into his lap. Nash buried his nose in her hair, snuggling against her. "I won't let anything happen to you, Van. I'm here for you."

"I know," she whispered.

* * * *

On the drive home, Vanessa's phone rang. The call Vanessa had been dreading finally came. "Mama?"

"Hello, Vanessa."

"How are you, Mama?"

"You're quite aware of how I am."

"No, you need to tell me." Vanessa wasn't in the mood to play games. Her mom was upset by the tone of her voice. *Ro wasted no time calling her.*

"Me? I am fine. Your sister … not so much. Rosa called me earlier and told me about your conversation. What happened, Vanessa? Why are you shutting her out?"

Vanessa glanced in the rearview mirror to see the Ferrari behind her. Nash had agreed with her. Keep Rosa safe. "I'm not, Mama. She never let me finish speaking. You know how Ro is. When she's mad, you can't get her to listen. I'm waiting till she calms down."

"True, she has a temper. So, why don't you tell me what you would've said."

Vanessa's mind raced, not having thought of an excuse. "I'm driving, Mama. It's hard to talk."

"Oh, you are in the car. Are you almost home? Call me back when you're in your apartment."

Vanessa bought a short reprieve and, luckily, Nash was following her home. They could decide what to say together before she returned the call.

The Ferrari pulled up next to her Mustang and Nash hopped from the car in one fluid movement. Vanessa forgot how agile he was, although, he never hit the weights too hard. She loved his body, suddenly missing their intimacy. *And he's not hard on the eyes either. If all goes well on Saturday, we'll be back together.*

"Ready?" Nash stood at the side of her car. "I'll take you in, check the apartment and leave."

The walk to her place was torture. Vanessa tried to think of a way to tell Nash she wanted to sleep with him right this very minute, rules be damned. Yet, how could she tell him it wasn't a sign they were back together. Instead, she said, "Mama called, and I need to come up with something to tell her about Rosa. I told her I was driving and would get back to her later." *Much later, if I had my way.*

Nash entered the apartment first, walked through the rooms and ended up in her bedroom when he finished. "Everything seems good." He turned as she came into the room, and they bumped into each other.

"Van? What if we …" Nash pointed to the bed, and she knew he was joking. "And I won't hold you to a commitment or anything?"

"Yes." She breathed the word out.

"What?" Nash's eyes widened.

Vanessa slipped the straps from her dress down her shoulders. If Nash pulled them the rest of the way down, he'd find her wearing only black silk bikini underwear. She closed her eyes and waited.

"I probably shouldn't." Nash ran his hands down her arms, sending tingles through her body. "I need to get going."

"Nash," Vanessa whispered. "Don't leave."

The dress slid down her sides and dropped to the floor along with his t-shirt and shorts. His lips found hers as he gripped her backside, pulling her to him. Vanessa relaxed into his body, letting the moment take over and her problems float away. He lifted her from the floor and walked toward her bed, gently laying her on the mattress. They spoke no words, knowing it might ruin the mood.

Tonight, she'd be with Nash, and tomorrow, when she might have to deal with the fallout, seemed far away.

* * * *

"How far from home were you?" Renata asked when Vanessa finally made the call.

Nash had just left after they agreed on a Rosa strategy. She would much preferred to linger in bed but needed to return the call. "I had an errand to do, Mama. It's not late."

"Ten p.m. is late enough, my girl. Now, let's get to the reason I called. What happened between you and Rosa?"

"As I said before, she didn't let me finish. She hung up on me. Rosa was a big help while we were at your house. We got a lot done. There's not much left to do. I don't really need her help until the day of the party, but I doubt she will let me have my say after our fight."

"I remember you two worked by the pool for two days straight. Rosa seemed so happy. She's disappointed, Vanessa."

"I wanted to tell her Nash gave the okay for her to work at the gym when the kids are in school. She can make her own hours. We'll have her be our girl Friday, doing a little of this and that. Whatever needs to be done."

"She would like that." Her mom paused. "But you didn't get to tell her about the job?"

"No." Vanessa sighed. "Maybe you could, Mama? This week will be crazy. After the gala, the three of us can do something on Sunday. How does that sound?"

"Wonderful, but you should tell your sister about the job. It shouldn't come from me. I will smooth her ruffled feathers until then."

"Thanks, Mama. I'll let you go. Good night," Vanessa said, and they ended the call. "Thank you, Nash!" She pumped her arm. "I can focus on the event, then give all the time I need to them after it's over."

When Vanessa walked into work the next day, Nash was waiting for her. She dropped her gym bag in front of her favorite treadmill and had to pass him by to reach it.

"Hey, Peaches," Nash said as he wound his arm around her waist, pulled her close and nuzzled her neck.

"I came to work early to workout, Nash, nothing else." Vanessa pointed at him. "I was afraid this would happen."

"What? Can't a friend say hello and call his said friend 'Peaches'?" Nash lifted his shoulders.

"You're getting your sense of humor back." Vanessa poked him in the belly and he pretended to be hurt. "Now, if you'll excuse me."

"I plan to run, too," Nash said, following her to the treadmills. "Remember, I'll be watching over you until Saturday's over."

He said something under his breath, making it difficult to hear. "What did you say?" Vanessa asked.

"I said you make it hard." Nash turned on his machine and started a slow jog. "Have you brushed up on your self-defense? If not, go to our class tomorrow night."

"I'll consider it." Vanessa turned on her treadmill and focused on a spot on the wall. "No talking."

After a half hour on the treadmill, Vanessa slowed to a walk and down to zero, jumping off the back. She double-checked the machine had turned off, grabbed her towel and slung it around her neck. Nash had moved on from running and she spotted him at a multi-station workout center at the pull-down bar. She watched for a minute then felt a presence next to her.

"You should go back to him, Van," Missy said.

"We slept together last night."

"What?" Missy tugged on Vanessa's arm, so she'd face her. "You're back together?"

"No, it's …"

Missy nodded at Nash. "You couldn't resist. Hey, to change the subject, I heard the dresses will be delivered on Thursday. I can't wait. We have to try them on together. Rosa called here on Saturday, excited to start today. What time did you tell her to come in?"

"She's not coming."

"Okay … does it have something to do with what happened Saturday night?"

"Word travels fast." Vanessa stared at Missy. "It was a little scary."

"Little? It's a lot scary. We've never had anyone break in here."

"If you ask me, he wasn't searching for money. I'm still trying to figure out why he came inside after hours. He said he was looking for Victor. Maybe he was."

"Look, Van. I don't have too many details about this fight or why Nash had to make it happen so quickly. But think. If Victor was in the boxing room and this kid found him, maybe he was supposed to mess him up or threaten him." Missy made fists and pretended to fight. "Then Victor couldn't be ringside to help C.J. It would give the other side an unfair advantage."

"I never thought of that. Thanks for the input." Vanessa rubbed her chin. "This will be quite the week for Gill's Gym."

"The RSVP's are pouring in. We may have to decline people who wait too long. I heard it's being called the Orange Ball."

"Really? There isn't any dancing, just dinner, gambling and the fight. But, we'll take all the publicity we can get. Rosa and I stuck with a generic name since we didn't have time to brainstorm. Gill's Charity Event, An Evening at Casino Royale."

"Not bad, but this thing is taking on a life of its own." Missy patted Vanessa's arm. "I'll unlock the doors."

"Yeah … sure," Vanessa said as she mulled over what Missy had said. She walked toward the multi-station when it appeared Nash had finished. "Nash, I'm going up to shower and dress for the day."

"And you want me to come?" He lifted a brow.

"No, be serious." Vanessa placed her hands on her hips. "Missy had an interesting theory, and I don't want to discuss it here. I'll come to your office when I'm ready."

"I'll go up with you. I probably don't need a shower …"

"Oh, you do." Vanessa laughed.

They climbed the stairs, parting ways at the top. Vanessa quickly showered and dressed, dissecting every detail of Cord's visit. She hoped Nash hadn't lingered in the shower. He tended to lose track of time. When she entered his office, he sat behind his desk, his hair still wet.

"We may be examining this from the wrong angle, Nash." Vanessa plopped in a chair. "Maybe Cord was sent to harm Victor, not get intel."

Nash stared at her in disbelief. "You said Missy thought of this?"

"Yes, it's her theory."

"I get it. No Victor. No win for us. Robbie wouldn't see his dad on the opposite side of the ring, and C.J. wouldn't have his trainer."

"One way to put the odds in their favor."

Nash rubbed his face. "Nothing is ever simple."

"Trying to rescue Robbie is beyond simple, Nash. Now you've put the plan into motion, don't back down or get scared off. We can do this."

"We? Van, I told you a hundred times …"

"Don't get involved. I'm aware."

* * * *

Vanessa glanced up from her computer to find Missy in the doorway. "They're here!" she cried, holding up a large box. "I can't believe it's Thursday already. This week has flown by. "Call your sister and tell her to come over."

"Do you mind if you call?" Vanessa dropped her head.

"Oh. Still not speaking? I thought after four days your fight had blown over."

"Not exactly. I'll make it right after the gala."

"I'll call, but let's not wait to look at the dresses."

Vanessa hopped from her chair. "Deal. You do the honors."

They pulled three dresses on hangers with dry clean bags over them from individual white boxes inside the big one. Each had a name taped to the plastic. Vanessa took Rosa's and placed it aside. It would look perfect on her sister, a deep peach color with a fitted bodice, rounded neckline and A-line skirt. It had tiny crystals attached to the top portion. When she moved, the light would catch them and give off a sparkle. "Would you mind taking Rosa's dress to the downstairs office when you leave, Missy?"

"Wow. You really don't want to see her." Missy teased. "Oh my gosh, your dress! You will look sexy awesome."

"Sexy awesome?" Vanessa closed one eye. "Did you just make that up?"

"Yes, I didn't have words." Missy laughed.

The halter top dress had wide straps attached to the bra cups which did not come together until almost the waistline. It had a sweeping floor-length skirt with a small train and one side was cut to mid-thigh. Both women's gowns were identical in color, Gill's Gym orange. The fabric shimmered in the light. Missy's dress featured an off-the-shoulder sleeve with a sweetheart bust, fitted to the knees with a flair of the skirt from there.

Kade had sent boxes of shoes, strappy nude color high heel sandals. A note said to mention the designer if possible, only known as Jordan. He added Nash would take care of the jewelry department. If they had any problems, call immediately, and Kade would tell them of a trusted tailor in Miami.

After the fashion show, Missy gathered up her things. "This is exciting, Van. I'm so sorry Rosa wasn't here to join us."

"Me, too, Missy." Vanessa shook her head. "Me, too."

CHAPTER ELEVEN

Nash straightened his orange tie before heading up to Vanessa's apartment. He patted the pocket holding the necklace, one piece he'd held back after letting Missy and Van choose earrings and bracelets. One last check in the car's mirror, then he opened the door. They'd planned to get to the venue early to make sure everything was in order.

Cocktail hour at six, dinner at seven. The casino room would open at eight and close at ten for the fight. Afterwards, it would reopen until midnight. *Check, check and check.* Nash went over the details in his head as he walked down the hallway to Vanessa's apartment. He knocked on her door and waited.

"Coming!" The sound of her voice made his heart flip.

When the door swung back, Vanessa stood in an orange dress leaving nothing to the imagination just as he had ordered. Nash whistled. "Fits you to perfection, Van."

"Good thing it's hot in Miami." She joked. "But I may have to borrow your jacket if the air's too cold inside."

"Not a problem. You ready?"

"Yes, let me get my bag." Vanessa walked to a side table by the entrance. "You got nice weather, Nash. No chance of rain."

"Lucked out there." Nash held out the velvet box, waiting for her to return.

Vanessa's eye popped as she came toward him. "Nash! What did you do?"

He flipped open the top to expose the string of tiny, individual diamonds which would circle her neck. "Let me put it on you."

Vanessa lifted her hair. He placed the necklace and fastened it. "There. Now you're ready."

"I have to see." Vanessa rushed to the mirror hanging in the foyer over the table. "Oh, Nash, it's beautiful."

"I'm glad you like it." Nash offered Vanessa his arm, and she slipped hers though. "You will outshine everyone tonight. Did I tell you, you look gorgeous?"

"Thanks." Vanessa kissed his cheek when they arrived at the car. "And thanks for putting the top up on the Ferrari. I didn't go to all this trouble to get windblown."

"I thought of everything." Nash came around to the other side, hopped in and started the car.

"I'm a little nervous," Vanessa confessed.

"I am, too. Once the guys get here, I'll be okay." *Finn, I hope you make it.* Finn texted he'd try his best to get here by the start of the fundraiser. Out in California, he'd lose three hours coming to Miami.

"Ready to give the welcome speech?" Vanessa asked.

"I thought you were doing it." Nash glanced at her out of the corner of his eye.

"Nash Gill!" She playfully swatted his arm. "You're supposed to do it."

"I'm not good at talking."

"Yes, you are."

"Can you at least come up with me? Read the charity names so people know where their money is going?"

"Okay, you big baby."

"I thought it was big guy."

"In this case, it's baby." Vanessa nudged him and he smiled on the inside.

"We get through this, and we're back together, right?" He wanted to remind her one more time before the evening started.

"I'm ninety percent sure."

"What about the other ten?"

"It's my safety net."

Nash pulled into the parking lot of the exclusive reception hall on the ocean. The building had a Spanish vibe, beige stucco, red clay tile roof, arched doorways with outdoor corridors. Beyond the venue, the lush landscape took over, catching the eye.

As they walked to the building, Nash checked the alfresco dining area which had a three-tier Mediterranean fountain flowing into a rectangle pond as its focal point, surrounded by outdoor seating. To one side, a long, rectangular tent ran along the venue's border, also filled with tables for outdoor dining. Once past the eating area, the land opened to a full view of the ocean. They had set the boxing ring at the edge of the property so people on the beach could view the fight if they'd bought tickets. Vanessa had requested special VIP chairs set close to the ring for those who attended the gala and he approved of the padded seating.

"It looks great, Nash, doesn't it?" Vanessa asked.

"Kudos to us. We pulled it off."

"Come on. Let's see if everything's set."

"One more minute. Are the screens set up for beach viewing?"

The reception hall had a walkway which ran along the side of the restaurant down to the ocean. Corded off, only those who had tickets would be allowed special beach privileges. Screens were put in place to block the view of the unpaying public and set in a way only people with access could watch the fight. And if anyone still wanted to watch the fight, a pay-per-view could be bought for any mobile device.

"I'm sure the screens will be in place before the fight. I'll ask." Vanessa took his hand, and they walked to the entrance.

Greeted by the event planner, she had the couple follow her to the room where they would serve dinner.

"Just like in the picture. Thank you." Vanessa touched the woman's arm.

The room gave off an orange and golden glow. Low hanging crystal chandeliers, white linen covered round tables and gold painted padded chairs made the room feel luxurious. Hardwood floors and peach-colored walls added just enough orange for the right effect.

"The room holds six hundred people, but we kept the list to five-hundred," Vanessa said. "We've rented the whole place, so people can go anywhere."

"How many outdoor seats?" Nash asked.

"Close to four hundred," the planner answered. "Some may have to stand. Others may not want to watch. We do have folding chairs on standby. It's so beautiful here, I didn't want to clog the view with rows of metal seats unless there was a need." She waved her hand. "This way to the cocktail room."

"Good thinking." Nash noticed six bartenders getting ready behind the counter as they entered the room. "Is that enough?" He nodded at the bar.

"I think so. There are servers who can fill in as bartenders if the need arises," the woman answered. "We have five wine stewards over there." She gestured to another bar in the corner of the room. "If you turn and look behind you, we have a craft beer station where you can help yourself."

"I might stay in here all night." Nash chuckled.

"Picture servers walking around with appetizers," the event planner replied. "There's something for everyone."

Vanessa tapped Nash's arm. "What time is it?"

Nash glanced at his watch. "Almost six. Time to greet guests or should I say the ones who come on time. If they want to be fashionably late, they'll have to find me."

"Nash!" Chase raised his hand in greeting, followed by Beau, Gabe and Kade as the trio walked out from the bar.

"You guys made it." Nash gazed over Chase's shoulder.

"He'll be here, Nash." Chase clapped him on the shoulder. "Finn's had a rough time."

"He gets to join our special club," Nash whispered to Chase and moved on to Beau. "Are you packing?"

"We all are," Beau said under his breath. "Want to tell us more now we're here?"

Nash had his friends gather round him. He checked on Vanessa's whereabouts and saw her speaking with the event planner. "I'm helping Robbie Dorado escape from his handlers tonight. We'll hide him and his mother in a safe place and hope his entourage will go home to Cuba after putting up a good front of trying to find him. When he comes out of the ring, we'll surround him and escort him away from the area. Regardless who wins, we take over. Three on each side. His mother should have a front row seat. Robbie's to embrace her in a hug, and we walk them out to a waiting car."

"You have everything in place?" Beau asked.

"Yeah."

"It sounds too simple," Kade said. "What's the back-up plan?"

"There is no back-up plan," Nash growled. "That's why I asked for you to bring your guns, for the unexpected. My security team will be in place by the hall doors and in the car. Our job is to get Robbie and Angela to them."

"I'm in," Gabe said and raised his arm in the air. "We may not all be here, but we are one." The other four joined him and stared at each other inside the pyramid they made. "No matter what, we have each other's backs."

"Hey! Don't start without me." Finn's arm joined the others and Nash grinned at him inside the circle. The pyramid was complete.

* * * *

"So, this is what it feels like to be king," Nash whispered in Vanessa's ear at dinner. "The peasants come to me and sing my praises."

Vanessa pretended to swat at him as if shooing off a fly. "Stop it. You'll have me laughing and spitting food on the table."

"A queen can do what she wants." Nash winked.

"The night has been amazing, except for …"

"Rosa? She's been great at avoiding you." Nash nodded toward her sister. "Even sitting at the same table."

"Mama is trying to place a buffer between us, and I feel sorry for her. She's not enjoying herself."

"I'll give her some gambling money."

"She wouldn't take it." Vanessa rubbed her temple. "I gave Rosa the assignment of desserts and decorating the casino room. She did a nice job. I heard she came in earlier today to make sure they set things up the way she planned."

"She's been knocking back the champagne during dinner and it appears she's hardly touched her food."

"Great." Vanessa's shoulders slumped.

"Poor Missy is trying to move the champagne bucket, but Rosa keeps pulling it back." Nash chuckled.

"Don't give me any more details." Vanessa covered her eyes, then dropped her hand. "I'm sorry your parents couldn't make it."

"They had something going on in the Keys, planned for months. It's okay, I'll drive down next week and visit them."

"You're a good son."

"They're clearing plates. Time for our speech." Nash rose and offered Vanessa his hand. "You got the list?"

Vanessa popped open her bag. "Right here."

"When we finish, I'll invite everyone to go into the casino or wherever they wish." Nash slid back his chair and offered Vanessa his hand.

"The servers know to set up extra stations of desserts where needed," Vanessa replied during the walk to the front of the room.

Nash stopped at the podium and placed his arm around Vanessa's waist. "Good evening, everyone. We hope you are enjoying Gill's Charity Event and want to thank you for coming." He planned to keep it short, hoping he sounded grateful yet confident. People clapped when he finished, and Nash took it as a good sign. "I would like to turn the podium over to my partner, Vanessa Alverez, who will read the list of charities which will benefit from your generous donations."

"First," a voice shouted from the tables. "I'd like to make a toast!"

Nash cringed and felt Vanessa tense beside him. "All right. Please go ahead."

"To you, Nash! You are a generous man." Rosa held her glass of champagne in the air. "Everyone! To Nash!"

"To Nash." Some joined in while others stayed silent.

"Thank you." Nash bobbed his head. "Now, if …"

"And," Rosa yelled. "To the people who helped you set up this wonderful night. Oh, wait. There's only one person taking credit for this, my sister, Vanessa. Good job, Vanessa. Let's hear it for her."

Nash stared at Leo until the man jumped from his seat and pulled his wife from the room. A smattering of applause started, and he watched the Society rise to their feet. The mood in the room instantly changed as Beau called out, "Bravo" and Kade and the rest shouted with him.

When the applause died down and Vanessa finished reading the list, Nash invited people to enjoy the venue, telling them the place was theirs to explore for the evening. Everyone laughed when he said dessert would find them, so don't worry.

Renata wove her way through the tables to get to the podium as people filed from the room. "Vanessa, baby, Rosa didn't mean it." She grabbed Vanessa by the arms.

"I know, Mama. It hurts she did it here in front of all these people."

"She had too much to drink. I told Leo to take her home. She'll be sorry in the morning."

"I hope she has a killer hangover," Vanessa snarled, and took Nash's arm changing her tone. "We better get to the casino." She slipped her other arm through her mom's. "Nash will stake you tonight, Mama, and you better use it to gamble."

"Since it goes to charity, I'll gamble all night."

Nash escorted the women into Casino Royale, impressed by the opulence of the room and the array of desserts. Before Mission Impossible he would have viewed this as all fun and games. *Maybe James Bond and the Mission Impossible dudes didn't have it as easy as I thought.*

Rosa had done an excellent job creating the atmosphere he'd wanted. A champagne fountain was at one end of the dessert table while a chocolate one complimented it on the other. Soft lighting had been accented by strings of white light. White and black were the main colors with high-end crystal used for everything else. Nash made the rounds, speaking to friends, business associates, singles and couples, checking to see if they were having a good time.

After an hour, he slipped his earpiece into place, connecting to the Society. They knew the drill. Test the system, memorize the layout of the reception hall. They'd picked a meeting place earlier and would watch the fight together.

"Nash." Vanessa tugged on his sleeve. "It's time."

Nash knew what she meant. He'd arranged for the boxers to have personal space in two smaller conference rooms in the back of the building used mostly for business meetings. Vanessa would check C.J., and he'd make sure Robbie and company were good to go. He followed her out of the casino and down the hall. When they reached the rooms, he said,

"Wait for me. I'd like a few minutes alone with you before the fight starts."

"So would I." Vanessa nodded, and they entered their separate rooms.

"Robbie!" Nash slapped him on the back. "Ready to win the fight?"

"Did my father send you in here to spy?" Robbie seemed to spit the words out as he hopped off a table and looked Nash in the eye.

Taken aback, Nash hoped he was acting. "No, of course, not. I'm Nash Gill, the owner of the gym and the host of this event. We met at the hotel."

"Oh, right. You're the capitalist pig who thinks we can be bought. We came to this country to show you the opposite. I am Robbie Dorado, champion boxer. I will prove to the world who is the greatest."

Nash counted the men in the room. They would outnumber the Society by two. "I'm sure you are. Have a good fight."

"I always do." Robbie stared at Nash and for a second Nash thought he saw a look of fear followed by hope in the young man's eyes.

Shutting the door behind him, he found Vanessa leaning against the wall. "C.J. is psyched! The vibe in the room is great. I hope he wins." She walked toward him, orange dress shimmering in the light. "Let's go outside away from the crowd."

The couple slipped out a side entrance. Vanessa glanced over her shoulder. "I need to tell Mama I will still meet her and Rosa tomorrow."

"Is she staying for the fight?"

"I'm pretty sure she is."

"You'll see her then," Nash answered. "When are you meeting them? Do we have time for a quick breakfast? I want to see you, too."

"I'll meet you at the gym, but it has to be early, say nine?"

"I'll be there." Nash stopped at the outdoor fountain. "Are you happy with the dress?" He reached for Vanessa's hand and squeezed.

"I love it. It fits perfectly and feels like I'm wearing nothing at all."

"I like the sound of that." Nash moved her in front of him and wrapped his arms around her, both gazing toward the water. "The guests have a good view of the boxing ring and the ocean beyond. I could have never done this without you."

"I know." She teased.

"Can we be serious for a minute?" Nash hugged her to his chest. "I mean personally, not in business."

Vanessa turned in his arms, head tilted. Nash debated what to do. *Is she asking for a kiss? What the hell!* He placed his lips against hers, questioning if it was right. She answered back by deepening the kiss.

The fight would start soon but Nash wished it was over and he could whisk his girl home. He'd ask her to take him back and to never leave him again. *What am I waiting for?* "Van," he said as he pulled back from the kiss. "Please say we are back together. I'll do anything you want."

"Anything?" She lifted a brow.

"Yes," Nash said as he breathed out.

"I want my own gym."

"What?" Nash's brain scrambled. "You're bringing that up during our romantic moment?"

"Don't I deserve a franchise?"

"Yes … no … I want you with me." *There. I said it.*

"What do you mean you want *me* with *you*? As a girlfriend at your beck and call? Someone to hop in the shower with?" Vanessa's eyes flashed with anger.

"If you want me to give a woman a franchise, I will. Would it make you happy? Would you drop this nonsense of leaving our gym and going off on your own if I did?"

"Nonsense? Do you not hear me, Nash Gill? *I* want a franchise, not any woman. Me!"

Nash dropped his head. "I can't."

"Can't or won't?" Vanessa's hands flew to her hips. "We are back where we started, Nash. You don't see me as a business partner or someone who has the smarts to run their own gym. I'm good enough to work for you but not exceptional. Wasn't it the word you used for Terrell? He has *exceptional* business sense and will run the Carolina gym well," she mimicked. Vanessa dropped her hands to her sides. "You know what? I'm leaving."

"You can't." Nash grasped her arm and she pulled it from his grip.

"Fine! I do want to watch the fight, just not with you!" Vanessa stormed away and before Nash could chase after her, he heard a voice in his earpiece.

"Places, everyone."

CHAPTER TWELVE

Vanessa was mad. Fighting mad to the point of tears. She pounded the pavement as she searched for a spot where Nash wouldn't find her. *I love him!* Her mind screamed, and her heart tore in two. Yet, her logical brain won out again. *He will never give you what you want. Validation. Damn and double damn!* "Maybe I would've stayed if you thought I deserved my own gym, Nash. That's all I needed. I want you to believe I'm good enough," she whispered.

Hip hop music came over the speakers announcing the start of the boxing match. People swarmed onto the patio to find a seat. Beachgoers had taken position as close to the ring as possible. Bright lights flipped on around the fighting zone, illuminating the area like it was the middle of the afternoon. The cheer of the crowd added to the growing anticipation.

Each fighter had their entrance choreographed and music set to play as soon as they came into sight. Vanessa held her breath as she watched Nash and his five friends circle the perimeter of the ring. They carried guns and, in her gut, she trusted them to do the right thing. She sent a quick prayer to heaven for their safety and those of the fighters.

Vanessa watched from the edge of the crowd and kept her distance. Nash had told her to stay far from the action, but it wasn't the reason she did so now. She wanted a clear distance between them. One far enough away where she could keep an eye on him, but he couldn't easily get to her.

The music switched to C.J.'s theme song. A friend of his had written a rap about the Mack Attack set to a steady, catchy beat. A red flag with a black and white mean-looking bulldog wearing a spiked collar led the parade to the ring. Women carried red and black pom-poms and followed behind the flag bearer.

C.J. appeared on the huge screens wearing a red, silk boxing robe with a bulldog on the back. The crowd on the beach went wild. The lights flashed on and off as fireworks exploded over the ocean. Vanessa hoped he'd win, crossing her fingers and sending silent messages of hope his way.

Once C.J. entered the ring, the music changed to a song with a Latin beat. Robbie walked down the aisle wearing a blue robe with a Cuban flag on the back while women waved larger ones around him. Boos mixed with the cheers and Vanessa wondered what went on in the young man's mind as he walked to the ring. He had the weight of the world on him, and not sure which was worse. The fight or the escape.

The bell rang, signaling the beginning of the bout. Vanessa stood, mesmerized. She gazed around in awe, almost in disbelief. She'd helped pull off the event in less than two weeks, and everything was going according to schedule. The rounds ticked by and when the fifth one started the men were even. Each fighter took punches but gave them just as well.

"How much longer will this go before someone breaks out?" Vanessa said under her breath. "Oh! I spoke too soon."

Robbie suddenly took over, hitting C.J. over and over until he had him up against the ropes delivering an illegal low blow as the crowd gasped. The ref pulled him off C.J. and back to the center of the ring. He gave the signal to begin again. One more violent punch, and C.J. lay spread eagle on the mat. The ref's countdown began as shouts of "Get up" and "Not fair" rippled through the crowd on the beach.

"Come on, C. J." Vanessa balled her hands into fists. "You can do it."

C.J. struggled to rise, spurred on by the shouts of the people. He wouldn't stay down and pulled his head from the mat, gazed around at the cheering crowd then fell back to the surface.

The ref finished the count, walked to Robbie and held his arm in the air. "The winner!" he yelled.

Robbie had won the match and the people around her headed toward the reception hall. Vanessa wondered if his handlers forced him to land the illegal blow, but the fight was over despite the protests. Vanessa stayed behind to watch Nash and his friends at work. The thrill of seeing Robbie and his mom drive away to freedom would make her night and soften the loss.

Vanessa kept her distance but found a place to observe the ceremony. After the mayor presented the trophy and check to Robbie, he climbed from the ring. *Darn! I went to all the trouble to get the mayor here to present the trophy to the wrong guy.*

Nash, Beau and Gabe waited at Robbie's corner as he climbed down from the ring. They became the buffer on one side. Chase, Kade and Finn took up the other to escort him back to the hall. As they walked, the group stopped at the front row of seats to part and let Robbie hug his mom. The fighter wrapped his arm around Angela and pulled her into the circle of men. They closed ranks and continued toward the reception hall.

Instead of going back inside, the group stayed in the outdoor corridor of the building winding their way to the back corner of the parking lot. The area was darker than the rest, a place where valets parked vehicles. A good five feet of dense landscape ran along the border, so cars wouldn't be seen from the patio or outdoor dining areas. Vanessa stepped from where the sidewalk ended into a mulched environment of tropical plants, trees and bushes, keeping her eyes trained on the fast-moving entourage.

Music, chants and loud noises came from the other side of the trees, tropical flowers and vegetation. Distracted by the party, Vanessa almost didn't see it coming. Eight shadowy figures plowed through the brush as Robbie and his mom were being ushered toward the backseat of a limo. Nash and the guys were ready but outnumbered. Her heart pounded as she watched the struggle, unable to make out faces in the dim light. Then the unthinkable happened. Gunshots. A few quick pops and it was over.

Vanessa's hand flew to her chest. She took a step backward and banged into something hard and unmoving. A gasp escaped her as she turned toward what she'd hit. "Cord!"

"You know my name?" Cord grabbed her arm hard enough to leave bruises. "Let's get you out of here. We don't want you to get hurt, do we?" He tugged her along to the empty front yard of the reception hall. "Keep your mouth shut and you won't get hurt."

Cord threw her up against the stucco wall of the building. Vanessa admonished herself for saying his name, but he'd startled her. She planned to cooperate until her escape. The front of the venue was decorative with no real entrance. No one would spot them except cars going by on the street. The reception hall had low lighting installed throughout the landscaped area but still it was hard to see.

"Why did you bring me here?" Vanessa asked.

"How did you know my name?" he snarled. "Tell me."

"From Victor. He said you were a friend of Ricky's. Right?"

Cord spit in the grass. "A friend of Ricky's? No. He's a mama's boy. I'd never hang with him. But." He shrugged a shoulder. "I may now since his cousin won the fight. Who'd ever thought Robbie Dorado was related to Ricky? How different can two guys be? Did you know Ricky bags groceries at the local Food Mart? That's his workout for the day. Then after his shift, he picks up his uncle from work." He made kissing sounds. "Do what mommy says, good boy."

"Cord!"

The stern sound of another voice brought them to attention. Vanessa sized up the man, wearing a black suit and orange tie as if he'd been a guest at the party. She memorized his coloring and features. *White man, maybe six feet, muscular, brown hair...* He came closer to her and grimaced. *A space between his front teeth!* She recalled Beau's conversation about Cord. *Father is white. Mother Puerto Rican.*

"What the hell do you think you're doing?" he yelled.

"She's a witness, Dad. She saw what was going on in the parking lot. When I heard the gunshots, I thought I better take her."

"And do what with her?" Cord's father growled.

"She knew my name!" Cord ran his hand through his slicked-back hair.

"What?" His dad's face twisted into a contorted expression. "Who is she?"

"The lady from the gym. I ran into her the night I was to pick up Victor."

"Can't you do anything right? Your job was simple. Tell anyone who saw you that you were Ricky Dorado. You were there to pick up your uncle. Was that so hard, dumbass?" He raised his hand as if to strike his son.

"Please, don't." Vanessa cringed.

"Who are you to tell me how to handle my son?" Cord's dad turned to her. "He understands nothing else except a good rap in the mouth."

Rage built inside her, but she willed herself not to go there and changed the subject. "I won't say anything if you let me go."

Cord's dad crossed his arms. "Let me think about it." He stared at Cord. "If you'd told her you were Ricky, we wouldn't have this problem now. If you pretended you were concerned and were checking on her, she be inside the hall right now. Instead, we have a problem on our hands."

"I made an executive decision," Cord answered, puffing his chest out. "I tried to find Victor that night, and she showed up instead. What if she'd met Ricky? She'd know I was lying. I had a job to do, and it went to shit. When it did, I said I was a friend and got out of there. I never said my name."

"You don't have to tell me it went to shit, asshole. And, if you'd left without introducing yourself, how does she know your name?" Don pointed a finger under his son's nose. "Ever think of that?"

"Don! There you are." A voice came from the shadows. "I need to speak with you."

While someone spoke with Don, Vanessa thought she'd make one more plea. "Cord, I am sorry about your dad. He should never hit you."

Cord took a few steps closer and was almost nose-to-nose with her. "Never speak about my dad. Do you know who he is?"

Vanessa shook her head and pressed her lips together as her heart pounded against her ribs.

"Don Owens. Back in the day, he owned the neighborhood. He and my mom? They were the *West Side Story* when they met. Dad made sure no one got hurt or fought to the death because of that film. You ever see the movie? We watch it every year on their anniversary." He sneered. "Don and Teresa were the king and queen of the streets."

"They aren't anymore? What happened?"

"Dad calls it marriage. Five kids. But they're done with babies. He's getting back into the life and taking me with him."

This kid is spilling it. If Don finds out, I'm in trouble. Vanessa had to ask one more question. "This was your dad's plan?"

"He's the one with the connections, but I …"

"Cord! What the hell are you doing? Get away from her."

Cord stepped away from Vanessa and walked to his dad. "What's the plan?"

"There's been a change. Robbie and his mom got away." Don pointed at Vanessa. "So, we're keeping her."

No! This is going from bad to worse. "I told you I won't say anything."

"There's nothing for you to tell, sweetheart. You met me and my son. Big deal." Don lifted his shoulders. "We're way past that now. You're much more valuable than you think. You work at Gill's Gym. You must have some attachments to the people there. Hell, if I was Nash, I'd be banging you." His gaze traveled from her feet and stopped at her breasts. "Nice dress."

"We're co-workers," Vanessa answered. "Nash doesn't care about me."

"Well, if he doesn't, he needs his head examined." Don let out a cackling laugh. "Besides, I don't give the orders on this job. It was a group decision. You'll be staying with us for a while." He glanced at his son. "Get the car, Cordero," Don ordered. "I'll stay with her."

"Okay." Cord paused. "Then what?"

"Remember where you were to take Victor?"

"The abandoned warehouse?"

"We had it ready for him …" Don glared at Vanessa and lifted a shoulder. "The guest changes. Go!"

"The night I saw Cord at the gym," Vanessa snarled. "He was supposed to kidnap Victor. Now, this all makes sense."

"Too bad it didn't work out. You wouldn't have been in this position." Don chuckled. "Don't worry. We stocked a fridge, put a cot in there and turned on the water for the bathroom. It's deluxe accommodations."

"How long will I stay there?"

"Until they make the trade. You for Robbie Dorado."

* * * *

"Do you always travel with duct tape and rope?" Vanessa questioned Cord as he pulled her in the backseat.

"Yeah, put your hands behind your back." Cord wrapped the tape around her wrists. "If you promise to stay quiet, I won't put any on your mouth." He ran his lips along her cheek. "Promise to be a good girl?"

Vanessa nodded, too ill to speak. Her stomach rolled over, and she thought she might puke all over the seat. *No! Get it together. Keep your wits about you.*

"Lay down." Cord ordered.

The car ride seemed to go on and on, turns and stops, fast and slow speeds. Finally, they came to a complete stop.

Cord jingled his set of keys as he pulled Vanessa from the back of the car. Vanessa tried to take in her surroundings, but there was only one lamp in front of a metal door. It smelled like they were in an industrial area mixed with the scent of asphalt pavement. She gazed up at the old brick building which appeared to be three stories high. The only windows were above the third floor. The door slammed back against the outer wall, startling her back to reality. Cord ducked inside, came out with a lantern and turned it on.

The huge space held mostly empty rows of metal racks covered in dust. The company had left boxes scattered around the area, some still perched on the shelves. Vanessa gazed up at the moonlight coming through the windows around the top of the building. She'd never be able to reach them. *If I checked out those shelving units, I could build something.*

Cord dragged her to a corner of the room where there was a cot, table and lamp. He turned on the light and Vanessa heard the hum of a refrigerator.

"You thought of everything," she said in a deadpan voice.

"We set your space up by the bathroom." Cord tapped a door. "In here." He gestured to a mounted camera. "We can see you at all times. No one wanted to stay in this hot hellhole to watch you. But don't try anything. Someone can be here in minutes. We're always watching."

So much for building. "It's not too bad in here."

"Wait till the sun shines. You can tell me again tomorrow how great it is."

"You're leaving?" Vanessa glanced down at her dress. "I can't wear this until I'm released. Take off your t-shirt."

Cord's shirt sported a picture of a heavy metal nineties band, but anything would be better than the dress.

"No way. This was my dad's favorite band."

"Take. Off. The. Shirt." Vanessa gritted her teeth.

"Okay! I'll bring you a different one tomorrow. Don't mess with this." Cord slipped the shirt over his head, and for a skinny-looking kid, he had muscle.

"Thanks." Vanessa brought it to her nose. "This stinks. Bring me a clean one."

"You get what you get." Cord stuck his finger in her face.

"Do you ever do laundry?" Vanessa baited him and hoped to keep him talking. Once he got to know his captive, he may see her as a person.

"Since I moved out, I have to go to the laundromat."

"Not allowed to use the family washing machine?" Vanessa lifted a brow.

"My mom says it's best to not have two alpha dogs in the house at the same time. They get into fights."

Vanessa remembered Cord and Don had been arrested for fighting. "Your mom doesn't like fighting. I get it."

"She called the cops on us once and immediately regretted it. Cost us." Cord rubbed his fingers together.

"The money went to waste instead of being used for something better. So, I don't go home much. We keep the peace that way."

"Oh, sorry."

"What? You don't have to be sorry."

"It's hard to not see family when you want." Vanessa saw the expression on his face and realized she pushed too far. "Or it may be great to have your independence. Do whatever you want. See who you want."

"Exactly." Cord smirked. "And you know what? I don't want to see you. I'll be going. Enjoy the place. It's all yours." He held out his arms and twirled in place. "Oh, don't leave the lantern on too long. Only use it when you have to. You're not getting any more batteries."

With a flick of a wave, he was out the door. Vanessa heard the steel door slam and the lock turn. She checked her dress, trying to find a spot where she might rip off the long skirt and train. "Damn!"

The lantern gave off good light, and she carried it to a row of shelves, spotting a rough edge. "I hate to do this to you," she told the dress as she slipped the material over a jagged edge.

The metal popped through the orange silk, and Vanessa continued to tear until she had a skirt just above the knee. The slit was about a foot long but manageable.

Exhaustion and fear set in as she walked back to the cot. Vanessa threw on the t-shirt, sank onto the canvas cot, curled into a ball and sobbed until she drifted into a fitful sleep.

CHAPTER THIRTEEN

Things went sideways as soon as eight goons burst through the bushes. "Go! Go!" Nash yelled to Robbie and Angela, shoving them toward the open door of the limo. He turned to the oncoming intruders, ready to protect Victor's family.

Surreal was the only way Nash described the scene. Men, dressed to the nines, in black suits and orange ties, fought with his friends wearing the same attire. Outnumbered, Nash surveyed the area, deliberating who needed the most help. He could handle two, maybe three, of the guys while the Society took on the rest.

Hand-to-hand combat ensued, and Nash questioned if they should pull their guns and end it. Before he decided, one of the perpetrators fired a weapon in the air, called for everyone to stop and put their hands in the air.

Hell, no. Nash drew his gun faster than any of his friends and aimed at the man's legs, shooting his feet out from under him. A few more quick pops of gunfire had Nash scrambling for cover behind the limo as the shooting continued, then the sound of sirens made the offenders scatter. When the dust had settled, two men lay on the ground, writhing in pain with the Society standing in a ring around them.

The limo hadn't budged, and Nash pounded on the window. "Get going!" he yelled, glancing toward the street. If the cops arrived before the car pulled away, they would refuse to let it leave. "Step on it!" He looked at his friends after the limo left the lot and gave a crooked smile. "Anyone hurt?"

"I twisted my ankle," "I'm bleeding. I need a bandage," and other whiny comments came from them.

Finally, Chase said, "Nah, we're good. What about these two bad asses?" He cocked his head toward the two laying on the ground.

"Police are coming. They'll take care of them." Gabe gestured to the flashing lights. "I'll tell them to call for an ambulance, too."

Bruce hopped from the first car and strolled toward Nash. "What have we got here? Taking the law into your own hands, Nash?"

"No, they came out of nowhere, Bruce. Tried to jump us. Maybe they thought we were easy targets. Lots of money here tonight. Better call an ambulance." Nash jutted his thumb over his shoulder. "For them."

Bruce talked into the intercom on his shoulder as the other officers gathered round him. He directed two of them to attend to the wounded and tipped his head to see around Nash. "Those your friends?"

"Yeah."

"They'll state these men attacked you? The perps asked for money or jewelry or whatever you rich guys carry on you?"

"Yes, they will."

"Is anyone carrying a weapon?"

"All of us."

"Concealed weapon permits that the state of Florida accepts?"

"I believe so."

"You're all coming down to the station."

"Now?" Nash lifted his brows. "Can this wait till morning, Bruce? It's been a long night."

"Sorry. We have two wounded victims here and need the story." Another officer came up to Bruce and whispered in his ear. "Oh! It seems Robbie Dorado and his mother escaped, drove to the nearest police station and are asking for asylum. Know anything about it?"

Nash raised one shoulder. "No, but good for them." He heard an ambulance in the distance and would arrive soon. He thought he'd try one more time. "Bruce, I swear we'll come in first thing tomorrow. I need to check on Vanessa. Make sure she's okay."

"If she's not standing here wounded, or another ambulance wasn't called, I'm sure she's fine." Bruce glanced toward the edge of the parking lot and the gathering crowd. "Nothing to see here, folks. Step back. Go inside and enjoy the party." He gestured to some of his officers to secure the area.

"Shit! The party." Nash threw a hand in the air.

"Will survive without you." Bruce gave him a serious expression. "I don't know what happened here, Nash, but you better be ready to tell the truth when we get to the station."

"I shot the one guy, Bruce … in the leg. I don't know about the other one."

They stepped to the side as the ambulance made its way to the back parking lot. An officer distracted Bruce for a moment, and Nash managed to slip away unnoticed to get to his friends. He quickly informed them of what he told the police. "Stick to the story." He checked each man to make sure no one was hurt. "Anyone need to get in that ambulance?" After the shaking of heads finished, he asked, "Who shot the second guy?"

An officer had been applying pressure to the man's side and relinquished his spot to the medic who came with the gurney. Seeing the blood on the ground, Nash feared the wound was critical.

"I'm pretty sure I did, Nash," Chase said. "Ballistics can confirm."

"Let's hope he lives."

Bruce approached the group. "Leave your cars here. We'll take you to the station."

"Come on, Bruce. Some of these guys need to get home." Nash glanced at Finn. He was in the middle of his mission and needed every day possible to complete his task, especially after the phone call the Society had received the first day on the job.

"Okay but get in a line. I'll put a car in the front and back of you."

"So, we're going caravan-style?" Nash lifted a brow.

"This isn't a joking matter. Get in your cars." Bruce waved his officers over.

Defeated, Nash gave in and told the guys to get in their cars. He glanced toward the building and hoped Vanessa was inside having a good time. *Knowing her, she stormed out of here and ordered a car to take her home. Probably didn't stay for the fight.*

Nash slid into the Ferrari and pulled behind the first police car. The rest had rentals and since they stayed at his house and had come to the same place, three cars instead of five got into the line. He glanced in the rearview mirror to see Beau and Gabe behind him and recalled his earlier conversation with Beau. Perhaps Beau remembered, too, and reached out to Gabe. Finn was in the single car as he had to fly back to California. The look on his face when Nash told the guys they had to go to the station was priceless. Obviously, Finn felt just as he and Chase had.

"You're no help, Smith," Nash growled. He wondered how Finn handled the man. Frustrated and overwhelmed.

The police car in front edged forward, turned on its lights without the noise of the siren and headed out to the street.

"Really, Bruce? You're making us, the good guys, go to the station." Nash smacked the steering wheel. "The only decent thing that happened was Victor got his family back." He paused. "Hey, I did it. I'm done. Derreck gets his community center and Victor's happy. Mission Impossible no more."

The cars glided into parking spaces next to each other at the station. Chase ran around the back of his to get to Nash. "If we can get Finn out of here, let's do it. I have a plane ready and waiting for him."

"I'll talk to Bruce." Nash followed the others into the building and searched the area until he found him. "Bruce? Can I talk to you?"

"What's up?"

"Do me a favor. Check out Finn Larsson first. See if he fired his weapon. If he didn't, turn him loose."

"Okay, but the rest stay." Bruce turned to the group. "Finn Larsson?"

"That's me." Finn stepped up.

"Come with me."

"Are they questioning us separately?" Kade asked, after the two left.

"No," Nash answered. "He's doing me a favor. If Finn's cleared, he can leave."

"The rest of you?" An officer waved her hand as she walked toward them. "In here." She wore rubber gloves and held five bags. "You will put your weapons in here and mark your name on the outside."

After they surrendered their weapons, she left them alone in the room with pencil and paper to write their statements.

"I shot the guy," Chase confessed. "Should I write that down?"

"No, I did." Beau pointed at him.

"It could've been any of us," Gabe stated.

"Except Finn," Kade said. "He told me he never got a shot off."

"Good!" Nash ran his hand over his mouth. "Bruce will let him leave after he makes his statement."

The time ticked slowly and Nash watched every minute go by on the wall clock. "It's past midnight. Party should be wrapping up."

"It was quite the gathering," Kade said. "I should have the girls model their dresses in Jordan's first show."

"They were debating if Jordan is a man or woman," Nash said. "I said man. Vanessa guessed woman."

"Sadly, Nash, you are right." Kade hung his head and looked up laughing. "A rare occurrence."

"Very funny." Nash tossed a wad of paper at him.

"Aren't you supposed to be writing your statement on that?" Gabe asked.

"There's more paper."

"I feel bad for C.J.," Beau said. "Kid should have won. The last move by Robbie was a low blow. Illegal, in fact."

"Are you saying Robbie cheated?" Nash asked.

"They might have told him to do it or he wanted to show his loyalty, but yeah."

Nash smirked. "You might be right."

The door swung open and Bruce stood in the entryway. "Your friend did not fire his gun. Permit checks out. He gave a statement, and I let him go." He strode to the table and joined the group. "His story sounded pretty much the same as yours, Nash. What about the rest of you? Sticking to the story? Out of all the partygoers, they picked six big guys walking in a group to jump and rob."

"Can you believe that?" Nash asked. "I was just saying the same thing before you came in."

The Society mumbled in agreement.

Bruce narrowed his eyes and lifted one side of his mouth. "Yeah, right." He shifted in the chair and continued. "We got a report from the hospital. The one shot in the leg is fine after surgery to remove the bullet. We'll match it against your gun, Nash. Whoever shot the other one? You're lucky. He will live. After a few pints of blood, he's in surgery now and doctors will stitch him up. Good as new, I'm told."

"I'd like to pay their hospital bills," Chase said.

"Very kind of you." Bruce glared at him. "I recommend staying out of it. Did you all write your statements?"

"Yep." Nash nodded.

"One of my officers will interview you, and if everything checks out, you're free to leave."

"Even the two who shot those men?" Nash asked.

"You said it was self-defense." Bruce stared at him. "Definitely."

"Okay." Bruce hesitated and rubbed his chin. "I do have to agree." A knock came at the door and he called, "Come in!"

"I have the ballistics report, sir," the same officer who had escorted them into the room said as she handed him the paper.

Bruce studied it for a moment. "Looks like all of you fired your weapons. We must wait for someone to analyze the bullet removed from the second victim. See which gun it came from. I have an officer picking both bullets up from the hospital as we speak. You're lucky they did the surgery tonight." He stood and rolled his neck. "You're not going anywhere yet. I need to know who did the shooting, so I can ask a few more questions."

"Damn, Bruce! You said we could go." Nash glanced up at the clock. *Almost two.* He looked at his friends, and they shrugged.

Bruce stood. "I'll check and see how far along they are." He nodded as he left the room.

"Anyone got a pillow?" Beau asked, stretching his arms in the air, muffling a yawn.

"It's going to be a long night," Gabe said. "Let's try to guess who shot the other guy."

"I keep telling you, I did," Chase answered. "He was coming right at me."

"Wait a minute," Gabe replied. "I was steps behind you. I shot him." He paused, took off his black-framed glasses and swept his hand across his face. "I've never shot anyone before."

"Well, if you did," Chase said. "Thank you. You probably saved my life."

* * * *

Vanessa floated across the dance floor lost in the music. Her dark hair hung loose, and she tipped her head back to gaze up at her partner, feeling the strands tickle her back. His face, partially covered in shadows, did not seem familiar. She'd been certain she danced with Nash as he wore the same suit and tie. Doubts filled her mind as they circled the floor, and she struggled to break free.

His arm tightened on her waist, pulling her closer. The look in his wild eyes said he wanted her and panic spread through her body. She had to get away, slip out of his arms when he loosened the grip and use her self-defense skills on him. Yet, they spun and twirled on the wooden floor. The music never stopped, and no one noticed her distress.

The man's face came closer to hers. He ran his lips along her cheek and toward her ear. She thought he whispered something in her ear but couldn't make out the words. Vanessa leaned back to give him a questioning look, and he smiled. A gap between his two front teeth, startled her. She screamed.

Sweat poured from every ounce of her body as Vanessa flipped onto her side, unwilling to open her eyes. Convinced the dream was over, she fell back into a restless sleep.

* * * *

"Four in the morning." Kade shook his head. "We should be leaving a club or totally drunk."

"This is a first," Beau said. "Hanging out at a police station, sober."

"Hey, I got an idea," Nash said. "Since I'm on my mission, I'll call Mr. Smith for help."

"He probably won't pick up," Chase answered. "He's sleeping or if he does answer, he will give you one of those lame lines of his. There's more to it. Dig deeper."

"I get Confucius sayings." Nash rolled his eyes.

Kade crossed his arms across his chest. "Great. Sounds like a helpful guy. I can't wait."

"Who gets the next mission?" Beau asked. "There's only three of us left." He pointed at Gabe and Kade then himself.

"Good question," Nash said as the door swung open.

Five pairs of eyes locked on the doorway. Bruce entered, holding a folder in his hand. "I've got the report." He waved it in the air. "Nash, you shot the one suspect. The other assailant?" He glanced around the room. "Was shot by Gabriel Nichols."

"What?" Gabe jumped from his seat. "I'm so sorry!"

"Gabe." Chase stared him down. "The man will be fine. Besides, it was self-defense."

"Was it, Mr. Nichols?"

"Yes."

"You felt you were in danger of losing your life?" Bruce asked.

"Absolutely."

"You're all free to go." Bruce motioned to the door.

The five couldn't leave the room fast enough, but Bruce grabbed Nash by the arm as he passed by. "A word?"

"Sure."

"These men you shot are Cuban citizens. If we charge them, I don't know what will happen."

"I'll bet if you go to the hospital tomorrow to speak with them, they're gone," Nash replied.

"I thought the same thing."

"Case closed?" Nash lifted his brow.

"Probably." Bruce's shoulders slumped. "Now get out of here before I change my mind."

"Thanks, buddy." Nash grinned. "You have to admit it was an exciting night." He slipped out the door with a salute and rushed to the exit.

His four friends waited outside the door, giving a collective sigh of relief when he appeared and walked with him away from the building. They congregated in the parking lot, all speaking at once.

"Hold on!" Nash held up a hand. "Who's going back to my house?"

"Gabe and I had planned to stay until Sunday night, so we're going there," Beau answered.

"Kade and I are heading to the airport," Chase said. "A flight is waiting for us."

"Okay, two stay. Two go. I'll finish the night off at the gym, grab a couple hours there and meet Van for breakfast."

The guys had no idea Nash and Vanessa had fought but he had no worries. Vanessa would show up to tell him to his face she wouldn't go anywhere with him even if he was paying. He'd chuckle and nod, she'd cave, and they'd head for their favorite breakfast diner. *Yep, that's how it will be.*

CHAPTER FOURTEEN

Nash caught a few hours' sleep, showered and waited in his office for Vanessa to arrive. "She can't be that angry. We said we'd have breakfast before she spent the day with Renata and Rosa." He checked the time again. "Ten-thirty. We said nine. Shit, she's never this late."

His phone lay on his desk, tempting him to call her. "One quick call. She might have slept through her alarm."

It went straight to voicemail. Nash searched for Rosa's number in his contacts and prayed she'd pick up.

"Nash?" He heard the two kids in the background. "Is everything okay? And before you say anything, I want to apologize for last night. I don't remember anything past the salad portion of the meal. Leo said I was quite the spectacle. His words."

"Forget about it. The fight upset Van, but she'll be fine. She knows you had hurt feelings. You two will work it out like always. She only hoped you'd have a killer hangover."

"Trust me, I do. I've been up since seven with the kids. Life of a parent never stops. Hangover or not. Hey? Is Vanessa with you? Tell her we're still on for later. I will grovel at her feet if I have to."

"Van was to meet me for breakfast and didn't show."

"Oh."

"What does that mean?"

"Nothing."

"If you know something, Rosa, you better tell me. Last night was a shit show, and I'm not up for more."

"Robbie and his mom are safe, right? I heard about the escape on the morning news. Also, they mentioned a shooting. Were you involved? They never gave names."

"Yeah, but not without casualties on their side. It was self-defense, but the guys and I were up all night at the police station explaining why two men are in the hospital with gunshot wounds."

"Where was Vanessa when it went down?"

"I told her to stay far away from Robbie, but we had a fight and I lost track of her before the match was over."

"Oh, if you two argued, then I better tell you. We talked when we were at Mama's last week. I suggested, and only gave it as a suggestion, that sometimes distance makes the heart grow fonder."

"What in the hell does that mean?" Nash yelled. He didn't have time for games and his patience was wearing thin.

"I told her to not come into work or see you for a few days. You'd see how much you missed her and make things right."

"Great," Nash said in a sarcastic tone. "She did it *now* after what happened?"

"I agree it makes little sense. She'd never do it on a day like this, especially if she's seen the news. Let me try calling her. I'll get back to you."

They ended the conversation and Nash stared out the window waiting for Rosa's return call. It came within five minutes.

"Nash? This is strange. It went straight to voicemail, and I tried her twice. Van would never turn off her phone or let it die. She'd always stay in contact with Mama, even if she's mad at you and me."

"I don't like it either, and no offense, we're wasting time talking when I should be doing something."

"Sure. Go. Keep me in the loop. As soon as you find her, tell her I'm sorry."

After speaking with Rosa, Nash dialed Smith. "What does Confucius say now?" he shouted when the man answered. "Where is my girl?"

"I don't know."

"What do you mean you don't know? You always know everything!"

"I am sorry, Mr. Gill. I have my people on it."

"Your people?" Nash looked for something to punch. "Has this gone sideways, Smith? You finally lost your touch? Big man has all the answers. Keep the Society in its place. These thirty-year-old billionaire punks deserve to be brought down a notch or two."

"Nash," Smith said. "I will call you with any updates."

"You better! And don't hang up on me because I'm hanging up on you!"

* * * *

Vanessa woke with a start. The nightmare of a strange man who kept creeping into her dreams ended with the break of day. A breakfast smoothie would soothe away the panic she still felt. She rubbed her eyes, confused by the smells around her. *Body odor? Did I sweat during the night? It doesn't smell like me.*

Bolting straight up on the canvas cot, everything came rushing back. The fight, the shooting, Cord whisking her to the front of the reception hall where she met her nemesis. *His dad. My nightmare.* "Don controls him. Cord may think he's an alpha dog, but Don calls the shots." She tried to come up with ways to get to Cord to let her go as she scrambled off the bed and padded in bare feet to the small refrigerator.

A carton of orange juice, milk past its date, water bottles and a four-pack of yogurt sat on a shelf. She grabbed the water and a yogurt. Plastic spoons and bowls were on top of the appliance along with a box of sugary cereal, crackers and a bag of cookies. "I'm here instead of you, Victor. Be glad."

"Next stop, bathroom." Vanessa gingerly opened the door, afraid of what she'd find.

A row of five stalls ran the length of the room with sinks across from them. A few toilets had missing doors, some hung from a hinge. The linoleum was yellowed, and the wall tiles aged and cracked. A sign on the first door said, "Use this one." It appeared old yet useable. Setting her breakfast on a small table holding two rolls of paper towels, she willed herself to push open the bathroom door stall. After she finished and washed up the best she could, she dragged herself back to the main room.

Determined to not break down, Vanessa sat on the edge of the cot to formulate a plan. "Nash will figure out I'm missing, but I can't wait for him. I know you'll be looking, big guy." She gazed at the ceiling. "Dear God, help him find me if I don't get out here first."

Nash's words from last night came flooding back to her. She mulled them over in her mind. He wanted to give her a franchise. He'd said yes at first. "Then he said he wanted me with him. I took it as an insult, a control issue." Vanessa dropped her head. "It wasn't. You're afraid your going to lose me. It's the reason you never gave me a gym. You wanted us to be a team, in business and life." She pounded the cot. "Why didn't you come out and say it, Nash? And, why did I need to be kidnapped to realize what you *weren't* saying?"

Her hand flew to her throat, coming to rest on the diamond necklace. She'd forgotten she still wore it. "If Cord sees this in the light of day, he might take it."

Vanessa undid the clasp, rolled the necklace in her hand as she pondered where to hide it. "Thank you, Mama, for the Goddess body." She slipped the jewelry into one of the bra cups of the dress.

The outer door made a noise, and Cord pushed it back against the wall. "You made it through the night." He winked as he approached, holding up a jug of milk. "See? I care." He tossed an undershirt her way. "It's clean. Now give me back my shirt."

Vanessa stood to lift the shirt over her head but didn't like the expression on the kid's face. He grinned as if he was at a strip joint. "Turn around."

"Come on. I've seen you in the dress. Although it seems you made some alterations to it." He gestured to the skirt.

"If I let you watch, you have to do something for me."

"Take off *my* shirt?" Cord pointed to his chest. "You don't even have to ask twice. I got great abs."

God, he's irritating. Vanessa smiled. "No, I mean bring me something decent to eat." She'd start small, ask for something doable, then hope to gain his trust.

"Okay, McDonald's for dinner."

"Or a salad?"

"If that's what you want. Take the shirt off."

Vanessa removed it as slow as possible and grinned as the material uncovered her face. "How about a fan?"

"Damn, girl! You get one thing and now ask for the moon."

Vanessa crumpled to the bed, pretending to be upset. He'd get a good view of her cleavage and hoped she wasn't pushing her luck. She'd never been a crier or able to bring up tears when needed. A good shake of the shoulders and a crying noise were all she could muster.

"I'll see what I can do. Hopefully, you won't be here long. We'll make the exchange, you for Robbie, and it'll be over."

Vanessa lifted her head. "You think your dad will let me go? I can identify you. He's not stupid."

"It's not part of the plan to kill you," Cord scoffed. "Don't worry."

"Me? Worry? I trust you, Cord."

"I'll see you tonight." Cord pointed her way.

Vanessa watched his every movement and waited for the moment he'd go for his keys. He pulled one key on a string from his back pocket before shutting the door behind him. She threw her body back on the bed. "Can I knock him out? Distract him? If I get the key and escape, I have no idea where I am. What if I run into someone who'd drag me back here?"

* * * *

The call came to the gym.

"Nash," Carla, his weekend manager, said over the intercom. "It's for you. The caller won't identify himself but said you'd want to speak with him."

"Fine. Put him on." Nash hit the speaker on his desk phone. "This is Nash Gill."

"You have something I want," the caller said in a Spanish accent. "And I have something you want."

"I highly doubt it." Nash was about to hang up when the man spoke the four words he had been dreading.

"I have your girlfriend."

"Vanessa? Is she all right?" Nash tried to calm his pounding heart. "How do I know you have her?"

"Send your cellphone number to the one I give you." The man rattled it off and hung up without another word.

Nash fumbled for his phone before he forgot the numbers and punched them in. No one answered and after five rings he disconnected. "Shit!"

After a few minutes, his phone rang. He'd gotten a video from the number. "Video or live action?" He stared at the footage. Vanessa sat on a cot in some dingy-looking room. "Concrete walls. No windows. Wait! There are windows higher up. She'd never reach them."

Vanessa dropped to her back, staring up at the ceiling. *Her mind is working overtime.* Nash gently touched the screen. She wore a white t-shirt, covering her gown which looked like she'd ripped the skirt. "Hey, peaches. I'm coming. I'll find you."

The video cut out, and Nash swore. He couldn't get it back either. "I need help but not the police."

Nash dialed Beau, praying he'd pick up. He and Gabe might be at the beach or on the yacht or sleeping.

"Hey, big guy, how did breakfast go?"

"It didn't."

"Van didn't show?"

"No, and here's why." He quickly told him the details.

"I'll grab Gabe, and we'll be at the gym in fifteen. Don't do anything stupid until we get there."

"I won't." Nash paced the room, knowing he couldn't go down to the gym. His face might give him away. It'd be all over the news and may ruin his chances of rescuing Vanessa.

Voices on the steps alerted him his friends had arrived. Nash rushed to the door and unlocked it. Once they were inside, he locked it again.

"It was a good thing you had me do a background check on Cord," Beau said. "That's where we start. Gabe's studied the information I gave him so he's up to speed."

"Before we go over my deductions, tell us about the video." Gabe took a seat in front of the desk, sounding like a police detective.

Nash sat at his desk and waited for Beau to find a seat. "It's like I told Beau. It didn't look like a house, more like a building."

"Can you draw it?" Beau asked.

"I'm sure I can." Nash sketched what he remembered.

Beau studied the picture. "I'd guess a factory or a warehouse."

"Wait a minute!" Gabe held up a finger. He flipped on his phone and scrolled. "Beau sent me the info, Nash. Hope you don't mind. There. This could be helpful. Cord's dad, Don Owens, is a factory worker. We need to find out where."

"On it." Beau's fingers flew across his screen. "I sent this to my brother in New York, Nash. He's got quick access to our database and is ready to go at a moment's notice. He'll send a pic of the guy in a few minutes."

"Making the kid work on a Sunday? Nice."

"I'm glad you still have your sense of humor." Beau smiled. "Got it."

"Wait," Nash said. "How do we know the dad's involved?"

"Oh, I never told you. Blake also did a background check on Donald Owens. He's got quite a history himself. Five kids but didn't settle down until the third one. He finally married his high school sweetheart, Teresa, when he was thirty and got the factory job where he's worked for nine years." He turned his phone toward Nash. "Recognize him?"

"Hell, yeah! I talked to Robbie before the fight and counted eight guys in the room. He caught my attention."

"Being Caucasian?" Beau lifted his brow.

"It might be one reason, but he strutted around the room trying to appear important. What's his name? Don?"

"Yes," Beau answered.

"He's trying to get back into a power position. These men didn't contact Cord, they had a connection to his dad."

"You may be right."

Gabe had been silent and glanced up from his phone. "It makes sense. Working for a large company, you blend in. No one notices if you step outside the lines if you do it carefully. Don may even have contacts inside the shop."

"The place where Don works has a few old abandoned warehouses," Beau said as he scrolled through his phone. "The company built newer ones in their place. My information says Don's position in the warehouse entitles him to have keys to buildings, old and new. All we need to do is scout those locations and figure out which one she's in."

"Even if we pinpoint where Vanessa is," Gabe replied. "We have to be careful. These guys want Robbie back. From the video they sent, a camera is on

Vanessa twenty-four seven. I'd bet there's one outside, too. They'd see us coming a mile away."

"But." Beau held up his pointer finger. "The camera cuts down on the need for guards. It could take time to get to the building, which …" He looked at Gabe. "I have a feeling you've found."

"There are three empty buildings, and I got the addresses."

"Sounds simple enough. Let's go check them out." Nash suggested. He'd have Vanessa home by tonight, snuggled in his bed.

"Nothing's ever simple, Nash." Beau stared at him. "We need to borrow an old car, one that would fit in and not be noticed. We'll drive to the three locations and hopefully you'll recognize the building."

"I'm on it." Nash pushed the intercom. "Carla?"

"Yeah, boss?"

"Is Juan here today?"

"Yes, he came in for the afternoon crowd."

"Thanks. I'll be right down." Nash looked at his friends. "Stay here. I'll be right back. Then we'll head out."

"Remember, Nash, we're doing reconnaissance. We have to wait for nightfall to do anything major," Beau called after him.

"Got it." Nash bounded down the steps and headed for the juice bar.

Juan had a knack for juice concoctions, and the patrons loved him. Nash had let him invest into the bar until they were equal partners. Juan trained every manager before he placed them in the franchises. Having a stake in the business assured quality.

"Juan, my man!" Nash lifted his hand in greeting.

"Good morning or should I say afternoon?" Juan checked his watch.

"I have a favor."

"For you? Anything."

"I'd like to borrow that contraption you call a car."

"The monster?"

"Is that what you call it?"

"My wife does. She gets angry every time she has to ride in it and nags me to no end. Why don't you take Nash up on his offer of a new car? How could you turn down such a wonderful gift?"

Nash had to chuckle as Juan made a hand puppet to mimic his wife talking to him. "How about you accept the car and put it in her name?"

"She doesn't drive, Nash. I keep telling you that." Juan dug in his pocket and tossed Nash the keys.

"Aren't you going to ask why I need it?"

"No, I trust you."

"In that case …" Nash pulled his wallet out and threw five twenties on the counter. "Insurance." He threw the keys in the air and caught them as he returned to his office.

"You got a car?" Beau seemed impressed.

"Yep. Let's go. Car's out back."

CHAPTER FIFTEEN

When they pulled up to the first warehouse, Nash stepped on the brakes, put the car in reverse, spinning around in the parking lot and drove away.

"What are you doing?" Beau sounded frustrated. "We didn't check the place out."

"It's not it." Nash glanced over at him. "Look back at it. It's a one-story building. Van's place was at least three floors with windows at the top."

Gabe leaned over the seats. "Good observation. I'll check this one off."

"Give me the next address, Gabe."

"Let me punch it into the GPS."

The directions took them to a remote part on the other side of town. The concrete building fit the description Nash had in his mind, but the guys convinced him he had to see the last one. "We're wasting time!" he yelled as he pushed the gas pedal to the floor and peeled out of the second building's parking lot.

"We need a plan, Nash, before we go rushing in," Gabe said. "After we see the last warehouse, may I suggest dinner and a strategy session?"

"As long as we have her out by tonight."

"I agree," Beau said. "But after dark."

As Nash drove to the last place, Rosa came to mind. "Beau, Rosa asked me to call her. Should I tell her?"

"That's a tough one."

"Her family deserves to know. What if something happens to Van, and we never told them?"

"Renata will lose it at first," Beau answered. "But will find the strength to deal with the kidnapping. Rosa? You know her better than I do."

"We'll call from the restaurant. Gives me time to reflect."

The last place was a bust giving Nash a good feeling about the second one. Rage built up inside as he pictured Vanessa lying on the cot in a dirty t-shirt and her dress from the party. He'd left her there. *We'll get you out of that dirty warehouse if it's the last thing I do.* After parking in the restaurant's lot, he pulled his phone from his pocket. "Shit! I got a message." He read it aloud. "Exchange goes down tonight."

"We don't even know where Robbie is," Beau said. "No one knows about the kidnapping but us. I hate to say this, Nash, but we may need to call Victor."

"No! We keep his family out of it until we're desperate." Nash flung the door of the restaurant back almost hitting his friends. "We get Van out sooner rather than later."

They got a table in a back corner far from the crowd and ordered. The server arrived with the food as Nash's phone rang. "Nash Gill," he said.

"I will tell you the instruction once. Do not bring police or any of your friends. Bring Robbie to the place where the fight was held. Have him stand alone in the front of the building. When we see him, someone will recover him and replace him with your girlfriend. Once we drive away, only then may you retrieve her."

"What time?"

"Eleven o'clock."

Nash hung up and relayed the message to Beau and Gabe.

"I have an idea," Beau said. "Here's what we need to do. First, we rent three nondescript black cars. One of us watches the Owens house and follows Don. I have a feeling they've given him the job of bringing

Vanessa to the exchange. Another one of us waits at the reception hall where Nash had the party."

"And the other goes to the warehouse and waits for Don to show up," Nash replied. "I want that job."

Gabe looked at Beau. "I don't care. You pick."

"I'm better at tailing people. If he drives to the warehouse, I'll be Nash's back-up. You take the party center. After we finish eating, let's return Juan's car and order those rentals."

"I'm on it." Nash sent a few texts. "Cars are being delivered to the gym as we speak."

"Before we go, I want to say something." Gabe fidgeted with the side of his glasses. "Thanks for including me."

Beau glanced at Nash. "That makes little sense, Gabe. You're always included," he said.

"You're right," Gabe said with a laugh. "It's just me. I feel like the outsider of the group. Something I need to work on, I guess."

"You're definitely not an outsider, Gabe," Nash answered. "I need you tonight."

"I hope I can live up to your expectations."

"Detective Gabriel Nichols? Hell, yeah." Nash said with a smile on his face. "Come on, you already have done a lot. Three heads are better than one as the saying goes."

"I'm pretty sure it's two heads." Gabe chuckled.

"Whatever." Nash waved his hand.

"Not to break up this bromance moment," Beau said with a smirk. "But you need to bring Victor in on this. Call him, Nash."

"He might be at the gym. Let's go."

＊ ＊ ＊ ＊

Victor greeted Nash as soon as he opened the door to the gym. "Nash, how are you?"

"I didn't think you'd be here today, Victor, but glad you are," Nash said and looked back at his friends. "We need to speak with you in private. Come up to my office."

"They told me to go about my business, doing what I do every day," Victor said as they ascended the stairs. "They will not allow me to see Robbie or Angela for their safety. They're in protective custody. The authorities will decide if they can stay in the country within the week. When we heard the verdict would come in so quickly, their lawyer was quite surprised. I assume you had something to do with it, Nash."

Nash shrugged. "I'm glad to hear." He entered his office and when everyone was inside, he closed the door.

Between Beau, Gabe and Nash, they relayed the story to Victor. The man remained silent. The only reaction was the shocked expression on his face. When they finished, he said, "You need someone to take the place of Robbie. I will do it."

"We hope it won't get that far, Victor," Nash said.

"They will have someone watching the reception hall. If someone doesn't stand in front, they may call of the deal. I cannot let that happen. I will wear a jacket with a hood and keep my head down. We are about the same height."

"We didn't tell you this so you'd put your life in a danger." Nash folded his arms over his chest.

"He can go with me, Nash," Gabe said. "If all else fails and he needs to show himself, it will be a last-minute decision. I'll let Victor totally be in charge. Whatever he decides, I'll stand behind him."

"Fine." Nash cleared his throat. "Now what about Rosa?"

"Call her," Beau said. "I'll go over details with Gabe and Victor while you do."

Nash rose from his chair and walked into the bedroom. How am I going to say this? Hey, Ro, Van's been kidnapped? "Damn!" He punched in her number.

"Nash! I thought you'd never get back to me. Mama's here, and we're both worried sick."

"Put your phone on speaker, Rosa."

"That bad, huh?"

"Just do it."

"Okay, we're both here."

Nash tried to break the news as gently as possible. Renata screamed out, and Rosa started to cry. He wished to wrap them in his arms, tell them it would be okay.

"Did you call the police?" Rosa finally asked.

"We're keeping them out of it for now."

"Nash! I've watched enough shows where they don't tell the police and it works out, but that's fiction. This is real. Call Bruce at least."

"I'll have her home in a few hours, Rosa. Don't worry."

"Fine, don't answer me. We trust you, Nash," Renata said. "It's the others who have me worried."

"Please wait for another call from me, and whatever you do, don't call the police. Can I trust you?"

"Yes, Nash … for now," Rosa answered.

"I've got to get back to the guys. We're leaving as soon as the sun sets." Nash ended the call and sat on the edge of his bed. He'd never felt this unsure about anything in his life. In the past, he'd set goals and reach each one at a time until he completed his mission.

Kidnapping wasn't in his pay grade and he had no idea what he was doing. Guilt filled him as he thought of the last time he'd seen Vanessa. They'd had a fight. He needed to find her and fix things.

Nash stared down at his phone, made a quick call and when he finished, headed into his office to join his friends. "Her mom and sister are pretty upset, but I told them she'd be home tonight. I've got to keep my promise. One good thing, it's the weekend. I don't have the regulars here at the gym. Missy would know something was up. She'd smell my fear."

Beau glanced at his watch. "Let's go. I'll sit outside Don's house and wait for him to come out. When he does, I'll contact you." He looked at Gabe and Nash. "Good luck."

"Same to you." Nash headed for the door with him and the others. "Act casual. I'll get the rental keys from my night manager and meet you outside."

The guys kept Victor obscured from view as they passed the glass-enclosed office and out the door while Nash made a big deal of talking to everyone as he walked by treadmills and workout stations, ending up in the reception area. After retrieving the keys from Carla, he strolled to the exit, calling over his shoulder. "I won't be back tonight."

Nash tossed Gabe a set of keys. "You two be careful." He turned to Beau. "Are we doing the right thing?" He placed keys in Beau's hand.

"I don't know. I'm torn between keeping it just us or involving the police. My brother's on standby. If anything goes wrong, I'll send him a text, and he'll phone Bruce. I assume he's working tonight."

"Yeah, the guy likes the night shift." Nash lifted his shoulder. "What can I say?"

"Do not make a move unless you discuss it with me," Beau said and slid behind the wheel.

"I won't." Nash tapped the hood of the car as he continued to his rental.

He had the farthest drive to the abandoned warehouse north of the city. Nash checked the time, wanting to be in place before the sun completely set. When he arrived, the large empty parking lot loomed before him. "I can't park here. They'd spot me in a minute." He scouted for a good position. "You picked a good spot, Don. Open on all sides, parking in front …" His eyes came to rest on a patch of overgrown bushes at the back corner of the lot. If something happened, he'd have to drive to reach the door in time, yet he could see from the area.

Nash drove along the edge of the parking spaces and backed into the shrubs, hoping the car would break though the branches. A few good spins of the wheels and Nash had the rental in position. "I'll be paying for the scratches, I'm sure."

Twilight faded into darkness. One lone lamp lit the door to the building. Nash settled in to wait but immediately sat up at attention. Headlights were coming his way. The car drove right up to the door and stopped in front of the warehouse. Even though it was hard to see, Nash was certain Cord hopped from the car carrying a bag.

* * * *

Vanessa jumped at the sound of the key in the door. Cord had broken his promise to bring dinner, and she'd given in and eaten a bowl of the sugary cereal with milk. Everything she'd planned, her careful strategies were never put into play.

"I got your salad," Cord said, walking to her.

"You're late."

"Hey, I'm sorry. Shit happens." Cord grinned. "You look like you worked up a sweat today. See, I told you it wouldn't be enjoyable." He glanced up at the windows. "Should cool down now. Sun's setting. Eat up." He threw the bag at her. "We're leaving in an hour."

"We are?" Surprised by the news, Vanessa thought they'd keep her stuck in this hellhole for a few days.

"Exchange goes down tonight."

"That was quick."

"We don't want to keep you any longer than we have to. Your people are bringing Robbie to a designated spot. Once we got him, I let you out of the car, and you'll stand in his place. Don't move. Don't try anything smart. We will tell your people when they can approach."

"Okay." *Sounds simple enough. Maybe too simple.* "So, your job is to take me to this place?"

"Yeah."

"I say goodbye, and you trust I won't ID you."

"You said you won't." Cord glared at her.

"No." Vanessa held up her hands. "I promise."

"Even my dad?"

"Yes, even him."

"Fine. Then we don't have a problem."

Vanessa popped the lid on the salad. "Thanks for this." She gestured with the plastic fork at the food. Even if she didn't feel like eating, she had to show her appreciation.

"We have an hour to kill," Cord said. "Any ideas how to pass the time?" He sat down on the cot next to her, wriggling close.

"I swear, Cord, if you touch me …"

"I won't." Cord hopped up and strolled around the area.

Vanessa didn't quite trust him and struggled to come up with a distraction. "What do you think is in those boxes left on the shelves?" After a long day in the hot environment, she'd kept herself busy by checking out the whole place.

"Good question." Cord walked down the row where a few boxes sat on a shelving unit. He yanked on one and it fell to the floor. "It's heavy, whatever it is." A whistle came from him when he peeked inside. "I can't believe the company would leave this behind."

"What is it?" Curious, Vanessa stood.

"Copper wiring."

"Isn't that what people steal from houses and buildings?"

"Box says fifty pounds. Might be worth a couple hundred."

"Take it, Cord. I won't tell. Put it in your car." The wheels turned in Vanessa's mind. *If he's distracted, I can slip out and make a run for it.*

"Are you going to help me carry it?" Cord asked.

"Sure."

"How stupid do you think I am?" He said with a smirk.

"I don't, Cord. You're just young."

"Shut up. Stupid. Young. Whatever. I know what I'm doing. I can come back for this stuff." Cord checked his phone. "It's almost time. Get ready. We're leaving in fifteen." His cell rang as he pocketed it. "Cord here."

The silence lasted a few minutes, and Vanessa watched Cord's face change to a look of surprise.

"You're sure. Text me the coordinates." Cord looked at Vanessa. "Change in plans. We leave now."

* * * *

Zoned in on the door to the building, Nash jumped when his phone rang.

"Nash, it's Beau. We have a problem."

"Go ahead."

"Don just left his house with his wife. She has dark hair like Van and is about the same size. She's wearing an oversized men's white shirt with an orange skirt sticking out below, light-color strappy sandals. He's trying to make his wife look like Vanessa. She's a decoy. I don't think they plan to bring Vanessa to the exchange."

"Go on and say it, Beau."

"She can identify them, Nash."

"She's a dead woman then. Good thing they don't know I'm here. Wait a minute!" Nash's heart pounded as he watched Vanessa come out the door and shoved into the backseat of Cord's car. "You could be wrong. Cord just brought her out."

"I hope you're right. Maybe Don assumes the need to show his wife before Cord arrives and convinced her to play the part. I've got to let the others know. Good luck."

Nash waited until Cord's car left the lot, started up the engine and followed him up to the main road. "Make a right turn, get on the highway and we're headed to the finish line." He held back until Cord completed the turn, then did the same. "Go straight. Head south. We're almost home."

After a few miles, the car didn't keep going south. It turned right at a street pointing to another highway.

"What the hell?"

CHAPTER SIXTEEN

Nash stepped on the gas, not caring if Cord knew he was in pursuit or not. "Where are you taking her?"

Cord's car wove in and out of traffic until they came to the Dolphin Expressway. Nash followed him onto the highway, heading west. "This makes no sense. If you keep going, the only thing out there is…" Nash smacked the steering wheel. "The Everglades." His heart jumped to his throat. "I can't lose sight of the car. Call Beau!" he yelled to his phone.

"Nash?"

"Beau, I'm headed to the Everglades."

"What?"

"Call Bruce. Tell him what happened. The little shit is going to kill her. Or thinks he is."

"Okay, I'm on it. I'm tailing Don, and it looks like he's driving to the reception hall. Gabe and Victor are already in position."

"I don't give a shit about that part of the plan anymore, Beau. Abort! Why should Victor risk his life now? Tell them to get the hell out of there. Get Bruce out to the Everglades. Tell him I'm heading west on eight thirty-six."

"Isn't it a toll road?"

"Quickest way in."

"I wonder if someone is already waiting for Cord and Vanessa. There may be more to deal with once you get there. I'm heading out to meet you. If you can, try to wait for me. Or at least, don't do anything stupid."

"Thanks, bro."

"You're welcome. Don will be in for a big surprise when he sees no one at the reception hall."

"Too late to put a mannequin in place of Robbie."

"Yeah." Beau let out a breath. "I'm about a half hour behind you, Nash. I won't be much help, but I'm coming. I've got to hang up and make some calls."

Nash concentrated on Cord's rear lights, keeping them in view. "Van, I'm right behind you. Don't give up. Hang in there."

* * * *

The car ride felt different from the one to the warehouse, fewer turns and stops. It felt as if the car drove at a high rate of speed but difficult to tell with her hands taped behind her back. Cord told Vanessa to lie down on the seat, and if she stayed quiet, he wouldn't put a piece over her mouth. The music blasting from the speakers would drown out anything she had to say, so she didn't talk. *He probably did it on purpose.*

Vanessa struggled to sit up and stay out of Cord's line of vision. She leaned low against the backseat to see out the window. They passed under a large freeway signpost containing three signs. One caught her attention, *Everglades* with the miles below. Her heart pounded as her stomach squeezed tightly into a ball. *How will anyone find me?* A tear escaped her eye and trickled down her cheek.

Her mind filled with wild thoughts as they drove along. The worst was Cord would shoot her and dump her body somewhere. *Not somewhere. The Everglades.* Silent prayers and goodbyes to her loved ones occupied her mind for the rest of the ride. Vanessa longed to ask Cord if he had the nerve to kill her, but the music blared for a reason. He didn't want to talk.

The car slowed, and Vanessa took it as a sign they were nearing their destination. Peeking out the window a sign said, "Everglades National Park Shark Valley."

She'd been there many times as a girl and knew Cord had pulled into the visitor's center. The music lowered as he slowed to a stop. The window rolled down, and Vanessa strained to listen.

"Anyone follow you?"

"No."

"A few miles down the road there's a campsite. Follow me."

The farther they drove, the darker it got. Moonlight struggled to find its way into the park. Vanessa buried her head into the seat to muffle her cries. She admonished herself over and over for uttering Cord's name last night. She should've played dumb. What a difference twenty-four hours made.

* * * *

Nash gambled if he should turn in the visitor's center or not. He pulled off to the side of the road, hoping Cord wouldn't see him. *If they don't come out in a few minutes, I'll go in.*

The area didn't seem the place to get rid of Vanessa although it made his stomach churn to consider it. After a minute, a car Nash didn't recognize came to a stop, turned away from him and drove further into the park. Cord's car appeared next, doing the same.

"He met up with someone. There will be more for me to handle." Nash glanced over at his gun lying on the passenger's seat. "It's you and me, baby."

Hanging back, Nash drove slower than he wanted during the twenty-minute ride. *Campsite?*

The cars turned right into a designated campground area and Nash kept pace after turning off his headlights. Once the cars ahead stopped, he pulled up to some bushes, grabbed his gun and got out, leaving the door open. Voices came from the other side of the shrubs.

"Get out of the car, bitch!"

Plans be damned. Nash didn't need to hear any more and raced around the foliage. Vanessa was in trouble. He watched her stumble as she emerged from the back seat, unable to catch herself. Cord held out his arms and stopped her fall. "Watch it, baby. I'm going to hand you over to these nice men now. We'll say goodbye here."

"Like hell you will!" Nash roared. He held his gun straight at Cord, poised to shoot.

"Nash!" Vanessa's eyes locked on to his and he saw the fear then relief spread through them.

Longing to rush to her, he held back, concentrating on her captor. "Where are these guys, Cord? I see no one." He shook the gun at him. "Let her go. Walk toward me, Van, slowly."

"You think you the big man?" Cord asked. "Think again."

Four men materialized from the darkness, making a half circle around Nash, guns aimed in his direction. Before Nash had time to come up with a game plan, shadowy figures dressed in black, faces covered with only their eyes showing, jumped from trees and underbrush like ninjas ready for a fight. It happened so quickly, Nash thought he was seeing things. They barely made a sound and took the perpetrators by surprise. They had the culprits' hands zip tied behind their backs, legs wound in duct tape and weapons in a pile before Nash blinked.

Nash glanced at the spot where Vanessa had stood, not seeing her. "Vanessa?" he yelled.

"Here!" a voice came from the bushes.

"I'm coming."

"No, I'm coming to you." She rushed around the vegetation, hands still tied behind her back. "I saw your car, and I thought…"

Nash's breath hitched. He'd never seen such a beautiful sight. Van, in a stained t-shirt, torn orange dress hanging in shreds below it, running to him. "Turn around." He ripped the tape from her wrists.

Vanessa faced him and fell into his arms. "Nash, I'm so sorry."

"What?" He hadn't expected those words. "For what?"

"Our fight."

"You were kidnapped and want to talk about our fight?"

"It's all I dwelled on in the warehouse. I thought I'd never see you again, and I told myself if I did, the first thing I would do is apologize."

"Okay. You apologized. Now we need to thank these guys." Nash turned to the spot where the men lay and counted four wriggling bodies on the ground, nothing else. "Where did they go?" He looked at Vanessa.

"Who? I didn't see anyone." She glanced at the men on the ground. "Oh! That happened fast. Four against one. The odds weren't in your favor, but you took them down."

She thinks I did this? "I only see four guys. No Cord. He got away and I will find him."

"It's okay, Nash. Let him go."

"What? Hell, no."

"I'll explain later. Trust me?"

In the distance, police sirens screamed, getting louder as they grew closer. Flashing lights caught his eye, signaling their arrival to the campsite. Two cars pulled up next to his, and Bruce jumped from the first. "Nash! Are you and Vanessa all right?"

"Yes … and how the hell did you find me?"

"Tracked your phone." Bruce smirked. "And, had a little help from your friend Beau. His brother pinpointed your whereabouts before we did."

Another set of headlights came down the road. A dark car parked behind the other two, and Beau emerged from the driver's side. Nash's eyes filled with tears. "Second best sight of the night."

"Nash!" Beau jogged to where he stood with Vanessa. "You gave me a scare going off on your own without back-up."

"I hear your brother Blake was with me the whole time." Nash chuckled.

"Not much he can do from New York City, man." Beau clutched Nash's shoulder. "It's good to see you."

"Good to see you, too."

"Is the moment over yet?" Vanessa asked, wrapping her arms around her waist. "I'd like to get out of here."

"You can leave," Bruce answered as he walked up to the trio. "But drive straight to the police station."

Nash looked at Beau then Vanessa, and they let out a groan at the same time.

"Really, Bruce?" Nash lifted his shoulders and threw out his hands. "After what Van's been through tonight? Let me take her home, get a good night's sleep and we'll come in tomorrow."

"Okay."

"Did you say okay?" Nash closed one eye.

"Only because Beau told me most of the story on the drive here." Bruce looked toward the men being led away by his officers. "Four guys? One of them your kidnapper, Vanessa?"

"No. I never saw these men until now." Vanessa shook her head. "It looks like he got away."

"Do you know his name?"

"No."

"At least you'll be able to describe him?"

"I think so." Vanessa shivered.

Nash wrapped his arms around her. "Bruce, come on, can't you see she's in shock? And besides, this isn't really your territory, is it?"

"They kidnapped Vanessa from the reception hall. The crime took place in Miami Beach," Bruce answered. "We got a tip on her whereabouts and followed through."

"I'm glad you did."

"And," Beau said. "After our talk on the way here, you cleared me, said I was good to go."

"Fine! Go! Before I change my mind." Bruce turned back to his men and shouted orders. "Collect any evidence. Scour the place. Make sure we leave no one behind. One got away."

"Beau," Nash said. "Could you do me a favor?"

"Sure."

"Call Rosa. Tell her we have Van, and I'm taking her to my place."

"They'll want to see her. I'll offer to get them. I'm sure they're in no shape to drive."

"Thanks." Nash stared at him. "What the hell." He grabbed Beau and pulled him into a bear hug.

"We're good, big guy. You can let go now. And you're welcome." Beau saluted and headed to his car.

"It was about this time last night they took you," Nash said, guiding Vanessa to the car. "What a hell of a twenty-four hours. I want you to tell me everything. He didn't hurt you, did he?"

"No." Vanessa slumped in the seat. "He's a confused boy trying to act tough to get his dad's approval."

"You're not going to ID him, are you?"

"No, but I will identity Don Owens."

"Hang on, Van. I need to call Beau." Nash waited for him to pick up.

"What's up? I'm barely out of the park. Are you guys okay?"

"Yeah, I have a question. When I told you to abort the plan, did you?"

"Do I listen to everything you tell me to do, Nash? If I did, I would've jumped off a cliff a long time ago. Bruce sent a car to the hall. I told Gabe to stay as a decoy until the police arrived. Hopefully, the Owens are in custody."

"That's all I needed to know. See you soon."

Vanessa looked at him. "The Owens?"

"Don had his wife dress up to look like you. They never planned to trade you for Robbie. Did Cord mention anything to you about the plan?"

"No," Vanessa answered. "He told me we'd leave in an hour then his phone rang. You should have seen the look on his face, Nash." She shook her head. "The message shocked him. But, he kept his cool. Said there was a change in plans, and we'd have to leave now."

"Thankfully, Cord never got word of what went down at the reception hall. I'm sure they arrested his parents before we got to the campground."

"Does Robbie know someone kidnapped me?"

"No, only Victor. He volunteered to stand in for his son. We kept the kid out of it."

"Kid? He's not much younger than us."

"He's Victor's kid." Nash grunted. "Whatever. I'm sorry, too, Van. I've been pig-headed and put you off every time you discussed a franchise. I thought if I changed the subject or told you how much I needed you, you'd get it. The thing is…"

"You love me and can't live without me for a second."

"Something like that." Nash chuckled.

"We're a team, a damn good one."

"Keep going." Nash reached out and caressed her cheek.

"No, I need to hear you say the words."

"You are capable, more than capable of running your own gym. Hell, you probably could run two." Nash inhaled deeply then slowly let it out. "Every time I pictured you not at main campus, I felt sick to my stomach and couldn't breathe."

"Aww, that's sweet." Vanessa took his hand.

"So, I'm giving you what you've wanted for two years, your own gym."

"What? You don't have to do it, Nash. Just saying I'm worthy is enough."

"Nope. Too late. Everything's in your name already."

"Where is it?"

"You'll find out tomorrow when you see the papers." Nash stepped on the gas, wanting to get home. It would be an hour before they stepped through the door. Luckily, Vanessa had clothes at his house, and he'd fill the soaking tub for her. She had a bit of a scent. He sniffed and wiped under his nose then felt a punch to the arm. "Ow!"

"I know I stink!" Vanessa laughed. "I was in a hot warehouse with no air conditioning."

"Sorry, I didn't want to say anything." Nash reached over and took her hand. "To pass the time, you're going to tell me what happened. Start right from the beginning after we parted."

The story helped the minutes go by, and soon Nash pulled into his driveway. Home never looked better. He'd called ahead, instructing the staff to fill the tub, make coffee, tea and sandwiches and have it ready for their arrival.

Nash jumped from the car, ran to the passenger side and took the sleeping Vanessa in his arms. A door opened, he thanked the person and rushed to the master bathroom. Vanessa stirred in his arms, snuggling against his chest. "Hey, peaches." He knew she'd wake at the sound of his pet name.

"Don't call me that," she said in a groggy voice.

"I will put you in the tub, with or without these clothes."

"No." Her eyes were half-shut, and she groaned.

"I have to. To put it as nicely as I can … you stink."

Vanessa's eyes flew open. "I do, don't I? Put me down. Go." She pointed to the door.

"There's my girl. I'll get some of your clothes."

"The black lounge pants and halter with the jacket."

"Okay."

Nash walked into his bedroom and let out a breath. Exhausted after last night at the police station and staking out the warehouse, he wanted to fall into bed. *Later.* He'd reserved part of his closet for Vanessa and each time they broke up she said she'd come for her clothes but never did. He found the outfit and pulled it from its hangar, hugging it to his chest.

Standing inside the walk-in closet, in the safety of his home, emotions took over. Nash sobbed silently, covering his face with his hand. Relief spread through him, yet he felt consumed by anger and guilt. His shoulders shook with each sob as he fought to gain control.

When Nash finally caught a normal breath, he decided to forgive himself. He looked in the mirror at the end of the closet. He had dark rings under his eyes but otherwise had little wear and tear. *Smith! I'm going to give the bastard a call. Get my pat on the head for a job well done and end it.*

The phone rang once.

"Mr. Gill."

"Hello, Mr. Smith."

"You have completed your mission."

"Yeah, with no thanks to you." Nash waited for a cryptic answer, but none came. "Hey, wait a minute. Those ninja guys … or women, you sent them."

"You didn't think I would let you walk into an ambush, did you?"

"You said you had no idea where Van was."

"At the time, no."

"How did you know to be at the campsite before me?"

"Some things are better left unsaid."

"Fine! What about Robbie and his mom. Will they get to stay in the country?"

"Most assuredly."

"Look, Smith, I know this worked out but don't give the remaining guys assignments like this. Things might have ended badly."

"Your plan was a good one, Mr. Gill. The unknown factor was Cordero Owens. What will you do about the young man?"

"Vanessa feels sorry for him. Can you believe it? He kidnaps her, and she wants to tell the police he had his face covered the whole time. Has no idea who he is."

"And his father?"

"Oh, she's going after him. She's not sure if Cord will like it."

"We will keep an eye on him."

"You will?"

"Yes, you have been through enough. Let's hope Cordero chooses the right path. If not, he may be arrested if he makes one wrong move."

"Well, you're a real pal, Smith." *Not really.* "I have to thank you for taking care of the paperwork for me."

"I was surprised to get your call yesterday. I agree to your terms and you will get a text in a few hours when it's ready."

"Fine, whenever." Nash let out a breath, happy with the outcome. "What about my other mission? The gym? I have no money to donate to the cause except what we raised at the charity event. That money goes to the high school. I've got nothing for the community center."

"Mr. Mills has received a very generous charity donation to the Nash Gill trust besides what you collected at the fundraiser."

"Wait! You made a donation?" Nash paused. "Smith? Are you there?" Damn!" He grabbed Vanessa's clothes and knocked on the bathroom door.

"Come in."

"Really?"

"Yes." Vanessa stood, wrapped in a towel, arm extended. "I'll take those. Wait for me out in the bedroom? We need to talk."

CHAPTER SEVENTEEN

Nash nervously paced the bedroom. *Does she want to tell me something bad? Why do I have to wait here?*

The door to the bathroom opened and Vanessa came out looking refreshed. "Thanks for waiting." She strolled up to him and took his hand, dropping the string of diamonds in his palm.

This is it. She's ending things. I don't blame her. I got her kidnapped. "You can keep this, Van. No matter if we're together or not."

"I wanted you to put the necklace in a safe place for now." Vanessa wrapped her arms around his waist. "I'm yours, Nash. No more break ups. I don't need my own franchise. I only want to be with you."

Those were the words he'd longed to hear for two years. He'd always thought she wanted to put distance between them. Every muscle in his body seemed to sigh with relief as he dropped his head to kiss her. "And, I'm yours."

Her sweet mouth took over the kiss, and if company wasn't on the way, it wouldn't have ended there. Nash lingered a minute longer, tugged her close and released her. "Beau texted while you were getting dressed. He's on his way with your mom and sister."

"They won't stay long if I let on how tired I am." Vanessa lifted the corner of her mouth and took his hand.

"If I know Bruce, he'll come to the station even if it isn't his shift to see this through. We better be there eight a.m. sharp," Nash said as they walked down the hall.

"Great. What time is it?"

"Two a.m."

"We'll be lucky to get four hours sleep."

Nash heard voices in the great room. "They're here."

"My baby!" Renata rushed to Vanessa when they entered the room and pulled her daughter into her arms. "Are you all right?"

"Yes, Mama, I'm fine. I did a stupid thing, but Nash saved me."

"She tried her best to save herself," Nash added.

"The kidnapping won't make the papers or any news outlet," Beau said as he approached to give Vanessa a hug. "It's one of the stipulations Robbie's men negotiated with law enforcement, especially if the police want them to leave quietly. Bruce checked the hospital and found the two wounded guys already left. No way to question them, they disappeared into thin air. The police will quell the rumor about shots fired at the gala, saying errant fireworks, and the unexpected blast caused the two injuries."

"What about news outlets who check police reports and scanners?" Vanessa asked.

"I had Blake scrambled all communication with Bruce. The police report will say Bruce and his officers were in pursuit of a stolen car."

"We still have to go to the station," Nash said.

"It's part of the agreement, Nash. We didn't get to talk much last night. Later, you and I will go over what you'll say. Make sure your story matches mine. Hopefully Bruce will stay true to his word and I don't need to give another statement." Beau looked at Rosa and Renata. "Agree? You know the true story, but it stays between us."

"If it saves my daughter?" Renata pretended to zip her mouth.

Rosa had taken Vanessa to the sofa and curled up next to her. "I feel like I'm in a movie," she said. "A heart-pounding thriller."

If only you knew. Nash nodded. "Good. We're in this together. Van, I'm sure you want to tell your mom and sister about the past twenty-four hours. I'll let you to it. Beau and I will be in the kitchen." He turned to his friend. "Let's grab a beer."

"Did you talk to Smith?" Beau asked as he sat at the kitchen island.

"Yeah, we're good. I'm done. My mission is complete."

"Two done, four to go. I know you didn't have much time to spend with Finn, but the guy is stressed, Nash."

"Tell me about it. After his phone call last Monday, I'm surprised he's still hanging in there."

"He'll pull it together."

"Enough about Finn, what did you tell Bruce about the kidnapping?"

"The facts" Beau answered. "Someone kidnapped Van. I followed the guy we identified through parking lot security footage. We got a read on where they held Van when they sent the video. Bruce will have a lot of questions, but after the threat from Robbie's men, the police chief has a choice to make. Keep the peace or blow it all to hell. Bruce doesn't get a say. He obeys orders."

"You're right. Although he's a captain and in charge of the night shift, Bruce has to follow them." Nash put his bottle of beer on the island. "Van doesn't want to ID Cord. I told Smith, and he said he'd keep watch over the kid. One wrong move, he'll make sure the cops arrest him."

"I'll put Blake on it, too." Beau shook his head. "Cord may want revenge, Nash. He might still come after, Vanessa. She's going to finger his dad."

"There's a way to find out if he plans revenge." Nash lifted a brow.

"Whatever it is, I'm in."

"My guess is he drove straight to his parents' house."

"They won't be returning any time soon." Beau tapped the counter. "Gabe said the police swarmed the reception hall parking lot."

"How is he?" Nash asked.

"Fine. He took Victor home and should be here any minute."

"Let's wait for him, include him."

"Include him in what?" Beau lifted a brow.

"Confronting the little piece of shit who kidnapped my girl."

"We're going after him?" Gabe stood in the kitchen doorway. "I'm in."

Nash walked toward the great room. "Van, the guys and I are going out for a while."

"What? Where? No!"

"It will be okay. We should be back in an hour."

"I'll drive since I've been there," Beau offered.

The three jumped in the rental, and Beau headed for Cord's neighborhood. "Look, there's his car. Parked right in front of his house. How stupid can he be?" Beau asked.

"Really stupid?" Nash closed one eye and studied the house. "I'll go to the front door, and you guys cover any other escape route."

Nash slid from the passenger side, strode up to the door and knocked. A little girl of about seven answered, showing no signs of surprise. She looked up at him with big, brown eyes. "Aren't you up past your bedtime?" he asked. She gave him a shy smile.

"Who is it? I told you not to answer the door, Maria." Cord appeared in the entryway, eyes widening when he spotted Nash. "What do you want?" He pushed his little sister away from the door. "Go."

"Been home all night, Cord?"

"Yeah."

"That's bullshit, but we'll go with it. You can tell the police the same story when they come to question you. It appears Vanessa doesn't want you to get into trouble. Your dad?" Nash lifted his shoulder. "She *will* identify him. Take her gift and do something with your life. You're being watched so don't make any wrong moves."

"Who are you? Are you from Mission Impossible or something? All up in my business?" Cord sneered.

"Yeah, that's exactly who I am. A man from Mission Impossible who has the means to make your life miserable. Consider what I said. Save yourself the trouble and head to the nearest police station if you think about harassing Vanessa." Nash stared at the kid and shook his head. "I don't get it."

"What?" Cord snarled.

"The good Vanessa sees in you. But, if she says so, I'll take her word for it." Nash turned to go. "Oh! One more thing. The police arrested your parents so don't wait up for them." He felt better as he walked to the car. Cord had been warned.

Beau and Gabe joined him at the car. Beau patted the top of it before sliding in the driver's seat. "Let's go home. Nash's mission is now complete."

Home never sounded better. Nash glanced in the backseat and then at Beau behind the wheel. "It's been a long night. I'm heading straight to my room and I suggest you do the same."

"Long night?" Gabe laughed. "I thought we were just getting started."

Nash walked into a quiet house. "Van?" He turned to the guys. "How did Rosa and her mom get home?"

"Uber?" Beau shrugged.

Nash made a noise in his throat. "They better not. All they had to do is pick up a staff phone and someone would take them." He shook both his friends' hands. "Good night. See you in the morning."

On the way to his bedroom, he noticed the guest room door was closed. Carefully, he turned the knob and peeked around it. Sleeping on the giant king bed were Vanessa, Rosa and Renata. His heart wrenched at the sight. "Sleep well." Nash gently shut the door and went to his room, set the alarm for seven and flopped on top of the bed. It was the last thing he remembered.

* * * *

"Nash?" He felt his leg jiggle. "You slept through your alarm. Wake up. We need to go to the station."

"No." Nash stretched his arms over his head and yawned.

"You don't have time to shower. Change your clothes." Vanessa gave him a shove. "I want to get the interrogation over and end this nightmare today."

"I'm up." Nash sat on the edge of the bed. "Could you pick out a clean shirt for me?"

"Sure," Vanessa said as she walked to the closet. "I ordered brunch for when we get back. Then we'll stick you in the shower and sit by the pool all afternoon doing nothing."

"Sounds good." Nash kissed the side of her head as she sat beside him, shirt in hand.

"Put this on. Shorts are fine. You don't even have to drive. Beau's taking us. One of your staff will pick us up from the station."

"I thought we were the only ones who still had to give statements." Nash rubbed the stubble on his jaw.

"We are. Gabe's already headed to the airport. Beau will drop us off and join him."

"Oh." Nash rubbed his eyes. "Damn, I never feel this tired."

"You're emotionally drained, Nash. We both are." She snuggled up next to him. "Rosa and I made amends. I guess getting kidnapped helped."

"Hey, don't say that." Nash wrapped his arm around her shoulders. "I called her early yesterday to see if she knew where you were. She thought you were with me and asked to speak with you. She wanted to apologize."

"She did?" Vanessa wrinkled her nose.

"Yes, she felt bad, really bad and had that hangover you hoped for."

"Poor Rosa." Vanessa laughed. "But I made it all better when I explained why I wanted her to stay away from the gym. She's also thrilled to accept her position at Gill's starting in August."

"I'm glad it worked out. Now I have to put up with two Alverez sisters at work." He teased.

"Nash!" Vanessa folded her arms, then giggled.

"Van?" Beau's voice came from the hall.

"In here, Beau. Come in."

"He's ready?" Beau leaned against the door frame and pointed at Nash.

"As I'll ever be." Nash grinned at his friend. "I hate to see you go."

Beau looked at Vanessa. "Mind if I have a minute alone?"

"Sure. I want to say goodbye to Mama and Rosa. They're almost ready to leave." Vanessa hopped from the bed and left the room.

"Did you get a text?" Beau asked.

"What? No." Nash stared at Beau. "Damn! You mean from Smith?"

"Yeah, this morning. Appears he's quite accommodating. We were busy this weekend as he says in the text and couldn't get to Carolina for our weekly meeting."

"He postponed?"

"No, it's tomorrow night."

"Really! On a Monday? That's Smith for you. I'll fly in and back out, although I enjoy staying at Chase's." Nash rubbed his face. "Shit! Nothing can go right. My mission's over and he's still pulling my strings."

"Don't throw a temper tantrum, big guy. I'm only telling you what I read."

"I really don't want to leave Van so soon. What was he thinking?"

"If I can guess? He's got someone watching her."

"Fine, but what am I going to tell her? Van, you've been through hell and need me by your side, but I need to leave."

"Tell you what. Take Monday off from the gym and you and Vanessa spend the day together. Fly in as late as possible. I'll arrange everything with Chase."

Nash got up from the bed and walked to Beau. "See you tomorrow night at Chase's." He slapped him on the back. "Thanks for all your help." His phone rang as they walked into the hall. Nash didn't want to answer but when he saw the caller ID, he picked up. "Derreck! What can I do for you?"

"Not a thing. I'm calling to thank you. I got an email this morning from the principal which said he received a large check from your event. He is overwhelming and grateful, and I told him air conditioning is a must." Derreck chuckled. "Besides receiving the charity donation, a generous amount of money was deposited in the Nash Gill trust. I don't think I can ever thank you for all you've done."

"You don't have to. Build your center and invite me when it's done."

"I will. And Nash? I know you'd never build a Gill's in Pittsburgh, but something needs your name on it. I plan to name the community center after you. Nash Gill Community Center."

"Hey, you don't need to do that. In a hundred years, people will say, "Who's that dude?""

"Don't worry." Derreck laughed. "I'll make sure they know."

"Thanks for calling," Nash said, feeling a little misty eyed. "I'll talk to you soon. Call whenever you need advice."

"You sure? I may install my own personal hotline."

"Funny." Nash smiled. "You're a funny man, Derreck." He ended the call to find Vanessa sitting in the great room, looking too fine for someone who survived a life-threatening ordeal. Nash wished they could stay home, but duty called. "Hey, Van, you ready?" He held out his hand.

"As ready as I'll ever be." Vanessa slipped her small, soft hand into his and squeezed. "We've got this."

Beau dropped them at the station and drove right back out to the street. On the way, they decided he should leave quickly in case the police changed their minds and wanted to question him more. Nash checked in at the front desk and the clerk told him to sit in the waiting room.

Bruce finally appeared, hands on hips. "Come with me."

"Both of us?" Nash asked.

"Yes."

Bruce led them to a small room with a large window. Nash immediately recognized the layout and leaned toward Vanessa. "That's a one-way mirror, Van."

"You're right, Nash." Bruce nodded. "We will bring in some people, Vanessa. See if you recognize any as your kidnapper."

Six men of different sizes, ages and race filed in and leaned against the wall. Nash felt Vanessa tug on his hand. She'd spotted Don Owens.

"Number five," Vanessa said. "I even know his name. Someone called to him from the shadows when we were still at the reception hall. Don, they said."

"Anything else you remember? Accomplices?"

"If it helps to identify him more, Don has a space between his two front teeth. He bound my hands behind my back, told me to lie down in the backseat and said if I sat up, he'd kill me. When I got to the warehouse, the person who drove me there wore a mask. I never saw him."

"What about a voice? Did the driver talk? Would you recognize it?"

"He barely talked. Mostly pointed and grunted."

Wow, Van, you had your story ready. I believe you. Nash placed his hand on her back for support. "You're doing good."

"Two men were involved in the kidnapping? That's all?" Bruce asked.

"That I saw. More seemed to be around the car in the parking lot. It was dark and hard to see. There were four at the campsite besides the guy who drove me there."

"I can't charge Don Owens with kidnapping," Bruce said. "It's part of the deal. Robbie's entourage will quietly go back to Cuba if we drop all charges. They'll give a heartwarming story of how father and son reunited and gave their blessing to the reunion. I hate to say this, Vanessa, the man in there goes free. We let the wife go this morning. She had no real charges against her, except she was with that idiot." Bruce nodded toward the glass.

"It's okay." Vanessa dropped her head. "Can we go?"

"Yes. Stay safe. I'm sorry this happened to you." Bruce extended his hand, and Vanessa took it.

Nash shook Bruce's hand after letting Vanessa go out ahead of him, walked to the door with a shake of the head, glad to leave the suffocating room behind them.

CHAPTER EIGHTEEN

Vanessa inhaled and let the breath slowly escape when she stepped out of the police station and into the morning sun. "I'm glad that's over."

"You're okay with Don being let go?"

"Cord will be happy."

"At least he won't have a grudge against you."

An SUV pulled up and Nash opened the back door. Vanessa slid in, greeted the driver and Nash slipped in behind her. He put his arm around her and pulled her close. "I texted the cook. The staff will have brunch ready as soon as we pull in the drive."

Vanessa felt his hard muscles twitch under his shirt and wondered if he was still anxious from what happened or truly ready to forget. She had mixed emotions over the ordeal and concluded her mom was right. She'd need to talk to someone, a therapist, not a friend. *I'll enjoy today and make an appointment tomorrow.*

The day went according to plan. Brunch on the patio, Nash in the shower and sunning by the pool. When dinnertime rolled around, they didn't want to move and had the staff bring the meal to the cabana.

"A perfect day, Nash." Vanessa peered at him over the top of her sunglasses. "And night to come."

"About that…" Nash fidgeted in his chair.

"What? No, don't tell me you have to leave."

"I'll be back before you know it. A quick trip to Carolina, and I'll fly right back."

"Why? Does Chase need to see you? He has a phone, you know."

"It's gym business. Terrell needs papers signed … ASAP."

Vanessa did not quite buy the story. "Want me to join you?"

"No, I want you to rest and relax. I'll be back here by nine, ten the latest. In fact, after dinner, I'm heading to the airport."

"Okay. Text me when you land."

Nash lifted his brow. "You're letting me off that easy?"

"Yes, I decided to trust you, and if you say you need to go to Carolina to check on your new gym, it must be important. I'll wait for you here."

"Thanks, Peaches."

* * * *

After a nap in a lounge chair, Vanessa wandered the grounds waiting for Nash's return. She strolled through the gardens until sunset and as she turned toward the house, a thought came to her. "I'm terrible. I have neglected Pepita this past week."

Her phone pinged, as Vanessa stepped inside the sunroom. She'd received a text from Nash. "He's on his way home, Pepita. There better be no detours."

The little lovebird chirped with delight when Vanessa approached the cage. "Pita, are you happy here?" She checked the bird's water which looked clear and fresh and noticed someone had filled seeds to the top of the food dish. "They take good care of you."

Pepita scurried to the door when Vanessa reached for the cage door lock. "Come on. You can fly for a bit. I'll scratch your head and then it's time for bed."

Vanessa showered the bird with attention, following her around the room to make sure it didn't get into anything it shouldn't. After twenty minutes, she stretched her tired muscles and yawned. "Bedtime, Pita." She offered her finger and Pepita hopped on. Vanessa carried her to the cage, locked the door and checked it was secure. From there, she went straight to Nash's bedroom.

While she waited for Nash, Vanessa thought a shower might refresh her. "A cold one to keep me awake." She giggled.

Afterward Vanessa slipped on a terry cloth halter top with matching shorts and jacket. She grabbed one of her books from a pile on the bottom shelf of the nightstand to keep her occupied until Nash walked through the doors. "I have a lot of questions for you, big guy, but I can wait."

"Did I hear my name?" Nash stood in the doorway, looking handsome as ever but tired. He wore a black t-shirt and jeans with the special stone she'd given him for their five-year anniversary hanging around his neck from a leather cord. His wavy brown hair looked as if he'd run his hand through it many times in frustration, but she thought he never looked better.

Even though Vanessa wanted him to join her in bed, she had many unanswered questions. One being, where did he really go? With every step he took, he came closer to the bed and the look in his eyes said she better start talking or he'd be joining her on the mattress. "Nash…"

Nash held up a hand. "Is it okay if I go first? Then ask me anything you want."

Vanessa swung her legs over and sat on the edge of the bed. She patted the spot next to her. "Come and sit."

Nash pulled papers from his back pocket and sank down next to her. Vanessa took in his scent, a mix of citrus and lime. They both preferred the aroma of fruit and it suited him. She wanted to drink him in, hold him in her arms and shut the world out. But first, she needed closure to start fresh again.

"This is for you." Nash placed the paperwork in her hand.

"What is it?" Vanessa slowly unfolded it to see official documents. As she paged through the pile, tears spilled from her eyes. "Oh no, Nash. You can't."

"Yes, I can, and I did. The original Gill's is yours. You own it, and you run it. I hope I can still work there if you'll have me."

Vanessa tossed the papers to the floor. "You didn't have to do this, Nash."

"I know." He winked. "I'm hoping one day you'll pass it down to our children."

"I will!" Vanessa threw her arms around his neck. "But no children yet. I have a gym to run."

"You do." Nash chuckled.

Vanessa pulled back and looked into his mischievous honey brown eyes. "I love you, Nash Gill."

"And I love you, Vanessa Alverez."

Vanessa pulled him down onto the mattress. She wanted him now and everything else didn't matter. "No more secrets. Right, Nash?"

"Right."

"We're a team now."

"Always were, but yeah." Nash rolled onto his back, and she snuggled against him. "I've missed you, Van."

"I missed you, too, but right now ... no more talking."

Nash had entrusted her with his prize possession, his favorite gym. He'd bared his soul and told her how he felt, why he had discouraged her for all those years.

She found his lips, the only ones she ever wanted to kiss, and knew they were finally in the right place.

The End

PREVIEW
FINN - THE $ECRET BILLIONAIRE
$OCIETY - BOOK 3 PROLOGUE

"Mr. Finn Larsson," the voice said over the speakers.

"I guess it's my turn," I said looking at my friends with a smirk.

Two had gone before me, like cattle to the slaughter, and I swore I would not become as frustrated or angry as they appeared during their missions. Chase wore a bandage over his right eye at the hairline, and I think he considered it a badge of honor from his assignment. An almost fatal car crash could have taken his life, but he shrugged it off.

My second billionaire buddy, Nash, the lighthearted one of the group, had become so serious I didn't recognize him. No way would this change me. In fact, when I got out of the interrogation room, I'd tell them I didn't need two weeks. I could do it in one. The man behind the mirror didn't scare me.

The man behind the mirror. We'd never met him. We didn't know what he looked like. Yet my friends and I agreed to put our lives in his hands and trust him. We only knew his name—Mr. Smith. He was now in charge of us, the Secret Billionaire Society, which started as a joke in college. Funny, but if truth be told, each of us made the Forbes Top100 list at one time or another in the past decade.

I had it easier than the rest of the Society, born with a golden spoon in my mouth as my dad liked to remind me. Gosh, I hated those sayings! Did I come out of the womb with one in my mouth? I think not.

My great-grandfather emigrated from Sweden and took up residence in Chicago, building a massive empire in real estate. Every time I had a complaint throughout the years, my dad would throw the saying and my great-grandfather's humble beginnings in my face. During my teen years, I'd learned to tune him out and continued to do a good job ever since.

I swore I'd make it on my own, but my dad's connections didn't hurt. My friends benefitted, and I'd hook them up with a contact whenever possible. I didn't want to be a part of Larsson Real Estate Corporation, so I created my own company, FLR, Finn Larsson Reality. Many people liked dealing with a younger version of a Larsson. Less stuffy and judgmental.

My parents expected my younger sister, Kirsten, and me to go to elite colleges. I picked Harvard. She chose Yale. Both of us went to school on the opposite side of the country from where we lived. We'd meet halfway between schools for visits when she came to the east coast, lamenting to each other and sharing secrets. Most people assumed we were spoiled, rich kids. What they didn't know was that we had so many expectations and pressures, it made for a stressful life. Mom and Dad groomed us since birth to be polite, use the best etiquette, tell no family secrets and excel at school and sports. I even had to find my way around swearing, a pet peeve of my mother's. To this day, I rarely curse.

My freshman year at Harvard, I met my best friend. I'd never had one before unless you count other rich kids who'd friend you one day and drop you the next. My college roommate, Chase Young, was handsome and driven. My parents disapproved of him and his background, never giving him a chance to show them who he truly was. Sure, Chase came from a broken home, but his mom had remarried, and was in a good relationship. I envied the calls he got from her. She'd call to check on him or to say hello. Somewhere along the way, sweet Maureen Rivers became a mom to me, too.

Chase and I hung out at bars many a night during our college days. The girls always seemed to find him, even if he didn't want to be found. Given the chance, I would have stayed out all night and partied, gone to class with bloodshot eyes and a hangover, but schoolwork always came first with Chase. We'd be back in the room by midnight. He impressed me to no end. No one drove him or cracked the whip to make him achieve. Motivation was his middle name.

The Society met at Harvard, a collection of six guys from all parts of the country who immediately clicked. My first real friends. Since then, we'd been a tight group, celebrating our birthdays on one chosen day each year. No matter where we were or what we'd been doing, we dropped everything and showed up at the designated time and place.

We had hired Mr. Smith, sight unseen, during a drunken thirtieth birthday party. Someone, no make that all of us, had an epiphany in the early morning hours. Time to contribute to society, we'd said, in a 'save the world' kind of way. Sure, we donated to causes, helped people out and supported charities of our choosing, but we wanted a hands-on approach where we personally made a difference.

Around two a.m. that night our buddy Nash found the Mission Impossible theme song and kept blasting it intermittently as we discussed this serious topic until a few of us tackled him and threw the phone into another room. After the random fighting subsided, we looked at each other in agreement. We needed a person like in the movie to give out assignments.

Beau, our tech guy, was on it before we could change our minds. He made a few phone calls, put the last one on speaker, and we interviewed the man or woman on the spot. Yeah, he had a man's voice but might have used a device to disguise it. Maybe Mr. Smith didn't want us to know who he was either.

After many hours of discussion, his answers satisfied all six of us and we hired Mr. Smith on the spot. Funny thing, he didn't want to be paid. He said he had his own altruistic motives and liked our plan. He wanted to be part of the team. *But.* There was always a "but" in negotiations, right? Something had to be at stake, otherwise we could easily back out. In our drunken state we immediately agreed to his terms. Mr. Smith would receive all we owned if we did not follow through with the assignments, every single one of us.

Before ending the call, Smith had instructed us to put together dossiers. A special courier would pick up the flash drives and deliver them to his secret location. Once he had the memory sticks in hand, he'd know everything about us. We requested separate assignments, but he'd set the parameters, make the rules.

When our new boss received and read our bios, he'd have instructions sent by another delivery person. Mr. Smith took no chances and didn't want us to use our cell phones, email, texts, or any technical means of communication to contact him. He'd be in control of communication. A message came within a week of receiving our dossiers. It said to build a soundproof room where we could meet, and the bunker was born. Blueprints were sent with specifics included, and Chase offered to build it at his compound. After completion, we'd receive our assignments.

We'd hang out in the outer room dubbed The Man Cave before Mr. Smith arrived, Chase had the best surround sound speakers installed and a huge flat screen on the wall. Music, video games or movies were at our fingertips. The bar was always stocked, food was delivered at intervals, and pizza only a dial away.

Today, after waiting an hour, a text sent to the six of us said Smith had settled in on his side of the bunker and we could now enter the room. We'd filed into the interrogation room with a one-way mirror. The guys on one side, Mr. Smith on the other. The tension reverberated through the room as we waited to see who'd be given the next assignment.

"Mr. Larsson?" the voice called to me again.

What happens next? Find out in *Finn The Secret Billionaire Society* Book 3 on: Amazon
Always free on Kindle Unlimited